CHARLES DICKENS
THE HAUNTED MAN
AND
THE HAUNTED HOUSE

ALAN SUTTON
1985

Alan Sutton Publishing Limited
30 Brunswick Road
Gloucester GL1 1JJ

Copyright © in this edition 1985
Alan Sutton Publishing Limited

British Library Cataloguing in Publication Data

Dickens, Charles, 1812–1870
   The haunted man; and, The haunted house.
   I. Title   II. Dickens, Charles, 1812–1870
   Haunted house
   823'.8[F]   PR4572.H3

   ISBN 0-86299-214-1

Cover picture: detail from A Moonlit Lane, with two lovers by
a gate *by Atkinson Grimshaw.*
Christopher Wood Gallery, London.
Photograph, The Bridgeman Art Library.

Typesetting and origination by
Alan Sutton Publishing Limited.
Photoset Bembo 9/10
Printed in Great Britain
by The Guernsey Press Company Limited,
Guernsey, Channel Islands.

BIOGRAPHICAL NOTE

CHARLES DICKENS (1812–1870). A man of singular imagination, novelist, editor, journalist, theatrical producer, actor and supporter of radical reform, Charles Dickens was one of the great Victorians. He was born in Portsmouth on 7 February 1812, the second child of John, a clerk in the Navy Pay Office, and Elizabeth, who were both extroverts and continually living beyond their sufficient but modest means, apparently more interested in themselves than in their children. He spent a happy early childhood in Portsmouth, London and Chatham, entertained by the macabre stories of his nursemaid, and later by his own wide reading, and developing imagination. In 1822 John Dickens was reposted to London, and his financial situation, already perilous, quickly deteriorated. Charles was unable to attend school for financial reasons, and after two years was sent to work in a boot-blacking factory, where he met with some of the rougher elements of London life. Meanwhile his father was declared bankrupt, and escorted with his family to the Marshalsea Debtors' Prison, while Charles had lodgings near his work, and visited the prison frequently. Fortunately, this sad state of affairs lasted only a few months, and later in the year, at the age of twelve, Charles was sent back to school to complete his education. He left school at fifteen, and by the age of twenty-three had established himself as a journalist and man of the theatre.

Four years later Dickens was a first ranking man of letters, a husband and a father. He had written the first of the *Sketches by Boz* in 1833, and, in 1836, *Pickwick* started to appear in serial form, to be followed by *Oliver Twist* (1838) and *Nicholas Nickleby* (1839). He had become editor of *Bentley's Miscellany,* and was receiving a steady income. He had married Catherine Hogarth in 1836, and had been devastated by the death, one year later, of Mary, his sister-in-law, whom he loved dearly. By 1839 he was able to move his impecunious parents to Devon, and to buy a family house in London. His writings were based on his own experiences and concerns: childhood problems and poverty pervade *Oliver Twist*; ideas of education and the theatre appear in *Nicholas Nickleby;* while in *The Old Curiosity Shop* (1841), he invokes memories of the beloved Mary, and *Barnaby Rudge* (also 1841) reflects Dickens' visits to Newgate Prison, his intimate knowledge of the London underworld and his political sympathies.

Dickens' experiences were broadened in 1842, when he made a triumphant visit to America. Although he was warmly welcomed, he did not like America, and was profoundly affected by his encounters with slavery and his visit to a penal institute practising solitary confinement. His criticism of American society was lightly veiled in the ensuing *American Notes* (1842), and continued in *Martin Chuzzlewit* (1844), another study of a disturbed childhood, which included a journey to the States. Dickens' support for radical reformers in England developed with his reputation, and he was frequently a public speaker for charitable institutions. He was particularly concerned with the plight of children, and was inspired to write *A Christmas Carol* (1843) after a visit to Miss Angela Burdett Coutts' Ragged School for deprived Cockney children, in order 'to present the poor in a favourable light to the rich.' This was the first of a series of Christmas stories which include both *The Haunted Man* and *The Haunted House*.

In 1844, after ten years of intensive work, Dickens took his family to Italy for a year's break. The family included five children and Georgina, Catherine's younger sister, who had lived with the family since 1842. Not unnaturally for a man of his temperament, Dickens missed London and his many friends, but he was stimulated by an experiment in mesmerism with Madame de la Rue, an attractive English woman who suffered from hallucinations. This relationship and the foreign environment exacerbated the relationship between Dickens and his wife, and marked the beginning of their final estrangement.

The next six years (1845–51) were busy ones. Besides spending nine months travelling and writing in Switzerland and Paris, Dickens was working as actor-manager of an amateur dramatic group, performing in London and touring the provinces. He was involved in an abortive attempt to establish a radical newspaper, but finally, in 1850, achieved his dream of producing his own journal, *Household Words,* which was an instant success, and employed many of Dickens' friends, his father and his father-in-law. Its purpose was to generate social awareness and to press for social reform. Two years earlier Dickens had opened Urania Cottage, a home for reclaimed prostitutes, under the patronage of Angela Coutts, and he retained responsibility for it as an unpaid superinten-dent. During these years he worked on *Dombey and Son* (1848), a study in selfishness, and *David Copperfield* (1850), a semi-autobiographical novel, which explored once more Dickens' own unsatisfactory childhood. In 1851 a series of misfortunes afflicted the Dickens' household. After the birth of their ninth child, Catherine suffered a nervous breakdown and was taken to Malvern for treatment. While she was away, first Charles' father, and then this last child died. Restlessness and concern for Catherine's well-being induced Dickens to move the family to a new home in Tavistock Square, while ideas of a new book whirled through his mind.

Bleak House (1853), was completed when Dickens was forty-one, and the end of that year saw Dickens give the first of his famous public readings of his own work. But the years of frenzied activity had taken their toll, and during that same year Dickens had been forced to take holidays in Europe, to avoid a nervous breakdown. Although he escaped a break-down, he continued to be possessed by a restlessness and feverish energy which he never lost, in spite of spending regular working holidays in Folkestone and France. *Bleak House* is a vast rambling criticism of the British legal system, and, like it, his two subsequent novels were satirical com-ments on Victorian 'systems'. *Hard Times* (1854), comments on the effects of mechanization on society and education, while in *Little Dorrit* (1857), Dickens explored the way in which people are imprisoned in their social milieu. Little Dorrit herself was modelled on Georgina Hogarth, who had lived with the family for the last fourteen years, a companion to Catherine, nanny to the ten children and beloved 'sister' of Charles. In 1857 Dickens, still involved in theatricals, took a production of Wilkie Collins' melodrama *The Frozen Deep* to Manchester, and invited the actress Mrs Ternan and two of her daughters to take the female parts.

Ellen Ternan, the younger daughter, was an attractive eighteen-year-old. Dickens fell in love with her, and within the year, in spite of criticism from his friends, colleagues and readers, had separated from Catherine, who moved out of Tavistock House. Since he now had three households to maintain, Tavistock House, Gad's Hill, which he had purchased as a country residence in 1857, and Mrs Dickens' new home in Gloucester Crescent, as well as the Ternans to support, Dickens needed to supplement his income, and this he did by making extensive tours to give public readings in England, Scotland and Ireland. At the same time, he continued his work as editor and journalist for *Household Words* until, through ill feeling, he changed publishers, and started producing a new journal called *All the Year Round*. The publication of the new magazine stimulated the writing of the next two serial novels: *A Tale of Two Cities* (1859), to establish a wide readership, and *Great Expectations* (1861) to maintain it. The first explored themes of death and resurrection against the violence of the French Revolution, while the second returned to thoughts of childhood and adolescent love in a plot involving mistaken identity.

In 1860, Dickens sold Tavistock House, and the next few years were spent at Gad's Hill, or in London or Paris, giving regular readings and writing *Our Mutual Friend* (1865), a study of material greed and mistaken identity. He also paid regular visits to Ellen, who was now living in Slough. The years were beginning to tell, and although he was now a wealthy man, he continued to press himself beyond the limit. In 1865, he suffered the first of regular bouts of trouble with his feet, as well as being badly shaken in a rail accident. However, in 1867, at the age of fifty-five, he set out for a victorious five month reading tour of the States, returning to a hero's welcome. But his final tour of the English provinces was not completed because of ill health, and in January 1870 he gave his last readings in London. He died on 9 June 1870 of a cerebral haemorrhage, leaving his final novel, *Edwin Drood*, unfinished. He was buried in Poets' Corner, Westminster Abbey.

SHEILA MICHELL

THE HAUNTED MAN
AND
THE GHOST'S BARGAIN

THE GIFT BESTOWED

Everybody said so.

Far be it from me to assert that what everybody says must be true. Everybody is, often, as likely to be wrong as right. In the general experience, everybody has been wrong so often, and it has taken, in most instances, such a weary while to find out how wrong, that authority is proved to be fallible. Everybody may sometimes be right; 'but *that's* no rule,' as the ghost of Giles Scroggins says in the ballad.

The dread word, GHOST, recalls me.

Everybody said he looked like a haunted man. The extent of my present claim for everybody is, that they were so far right. He did.

Who could have seen his hollow cheeks; his sunken, brilliant eye; his black-attired figure, indefinably grim, although well knit and well proportioned; his grizzled hair hanging, like tangled seaweed, about his face – as if he had been, through his whole life, a lonely mark for the chafing and beating of the great deep of humanity – but might have said he looked like a haunted man?

Who could have observed his manner, taciturn, thoughtful, gloomy, shadowed by habitual reserve, retiring always, and jocund never, with a distraught air of reverting to a bygone place and time, or of listening to some old echoes in his mind, but might have said it was the manner of a haunted man?

Who could have heard his voice, slow-speaking, deep, and grave, with a natural fulness and melody in it which he seemed to set himself against and stop, but might have said it was the voice of a haunted man?

Who that had seen him in his inner chamber, part library and part laboratory – for he was, as the world knew, far and wide, a learned man in chemistry, and a teacher on whose lips and hands a crowd of aspiring ears and eyes hung daily – who that had seen him there, upon a winter night, alone, surrounded by his drugs and instruments and books; the shadow of his shaded lamp a monstrous beetle on the wall, motionless among a crowd of spectral shapes raised there by the flickering of the fire upon the quaint objects around him; some of these phantoms (the reflection of glass vessels that held liquids) trembling at heart like things that knew his power to uncombine them, and to give back their component parts to fire and vapour; – who that had seen him then, his work done, and he pondering in his chair before the rusted grate and red flame, moving his thin mouth as if in speech, but silent as the dead, would not have said that the man seemed haunted, and the chamber too?

Who might not, by a very easy flight of fancy, have believed that everything about him took this haunted tone, and that he lived on haunted ground?

His dwelling was so solitary and vault-like – an old, retired part of an ancient endowment for students, once a brave edifice planted in an open place, but now the obsolete whim of forgotten architects; smoke-age-and-weather darkened, squeezed on every side by the overgrowing of the great city, and choked, like an old well, with stones and bricks; its small quadrangles, lying down in very pits formed by the streets and buildings, which, in course of time, had been constructed above its heavy chimney-stacks; its old trees, insulted by the neighbouring smoke, which deigned to droop so low when it was very feeble, and the weather very moody; its grass-plots, struggling with the mildewed earth to be grass, or to win any show of compromise; its silent pavement, unaccustomed to the tread of feet, and even to the observation of eyes, except when a stray face looked down from the upper world, wondering what nook it was; its sun-dial in a little bricked-up corner, where no sun had straggled for a hundred years, but where, in compensation for the sun's neglect, the snow would lie for weeks when it lay nowhere else, and the black east wind would spin like a huge humming-top, when in all other places it was silent and still.

His dwelling, at its heart and core – within doors – at his fireside – was so lowering and old, so crazy, yet so strong, with its worm-eaten beams of wood in the ceiling, and its sturdy floor shelving downward to the great oak chimney-piece; so environed and hemmed in by the pressure of the town, yet so remote in fashion, age, and custom; so quiet, yet so thundering with echoes when a distant voice was raised, or a door was shut – echoes not confined to the many low passages and empty rooms, but rumbling and grumbling till they were stifled in the heavy air of the forgotten crypt where the Norman arches were half buried in the earth.

You should have seen him in his dwelling about twilight, in the dead winter-time.

When the wind was blowing shrill and shrewd, with the going down of the blurred sun. When it was just so dark as that the forms of things were indistinct and big – but not wholly lost. When sitters by the fire began to see wild faces and figures, mountains and abysses, ambuscades and armies, in the coals. When people in the streets bent down their heads, and ran before the weather. When those who were obliged to meet it were stopped at angry corners, stung by wandering snow-flakes alighting on the lashes of their eyes – which fell too sparingly, and were blown away too quickly, to leave a trace upon the frozen ground. When windows of private houses closed up tight and warm. When lighted gas began to burst forth in the busy and the quiet streets, fast blackening otherwise. When stray pedestrians, shivering along the latter, looked down at the glowing fires in the kitchens, and sharpened their sharp appetites by sniffing up the fragrance of whole miles of dinners.

When travellers by land were bitter cold, and looked wearily on gloomy landscapes, rustling and shuddering in the blast. When mariners at sea, outlying upon icy yards, were tossed and swung above the howling ocean dreadfully. When lighthouses, on rocks and headlands, showed solitary and watchful; and benighted sea birds breasted on against their ponderous lanterns; and fell dead. When little readers of story books, by the firelight, trembled to think of Cassim Baba cut into quarters, hanging in the Robbers' Cave, or had some small misgivings that the fierce old woman, with the crutch, who used to start out of the box in the merchant Abudah's bedroom, might, one of these nights, be found upon the stairs, in the long, cold, dusky journey up to bed.

When, in rustic places, the last glimmering of daylight died away from the ends of avenues; and the trees, arching overhead, were sullen and black. When, in parks and woods, the high wet fern and sodden moss and beds of fallen leaves, and trunks of trees, were lost to view, in masses of impenetrable shade. When mists arose from dyke, and fen, and river. When lights in old halls and in cottage windows were a cheerful sight. When the mill stopped, the wheelwright and the blacksmith shut their workshops, the turnpike-gate closed, the plough and harrow were left lonely in the fields, the labourer and team went home, and the striking of the church clock had a deeper sound than at noon, and the churchyard wicket would be swung no more that night.

When twilight everywhere released the shadows, prisoned up all day, that now closed in and gathered like mustering swarms of ghosts. When they stood lowering in corners of rooms, and frowned out from behind half-opened doors. When they had full possession of unoccupied apartments. When they danced upon the floors, and walls, and ceilings of inhabited chambers while the fire was low, and withdrew like ebbing waters when it sprung into a blaze. When they fantastically mocked the shapes of household objects, making the nurse an ogress, the rocking-horse a monster, the wondering child, half scared and half amused, a stranger to itself – the very tongs upon the hearth a straddling giant with his arms a-kimbo, evidently smelling the blood of Englishmen, and wanting to grind people's bones to make his bread.

When these shadows brought into the minds of older people other thoughts, and showed them different images. When they stole from their retreats, in the likenesses of forms and faces from the past, from the grave, from the deep, deep gulf, where the things that might have been, and never were, are always wandering.

When he sat, as already mentioned, gazing at the fire. When, as it rose and fell, the shadows went and came. When he took no heed of them with his bodily eyes; but, let them come or let them go, looked fixedly at the fire. You should have seen him then.

When the sounds that had arisen with the shadows, and come out of their lurking-places at the twilight summons, seemed to make a deeper stillness all about him. When the wind was rumbling in the chimney, and sometimes crooning, sometimes howling, in the house. When the old trees outward were so shaken and beaten, that one querulous old rook, unable to sleep, protested now and then in a feeble, dozy, high-up 'Caw!' When, at intervals, the window trembled, the rusty vane upon the turret-top complained, the clock beneath it recorded that another quarter of an hour was gone, or the fire collapsed and fell in with a rattle.

— When a knock came at his door, in short, as he was sitting so, and roused him.

'Who's that?' said he. 'Come in!'

Surely there had been no figure leaning on the back of his chair; no face looking over it. It is certain that no gliding footstep touched the floor as he lifted up his head with a start, and spoke. And yet there was no mirror in the room on whose surface his own form could have cast its shadow for a moment: and Something had passed darkly and gone!

'I'm humbly fearful, sir,' said a fresh-coloured busy man, holding the door open with his foot for the admission of himself and a wooden tray he carried, and letting it go again by very gentle and careful degrees, when he and the tray had got in, lest it should close noisily, 'that it's a good bit past the time tonight. But Mrs. William had been taken off her legs so often —'

'By the wind? Ay! I have heard it rising.'

'— By the wind, sir – that it's a mercy she got home at all. Oh dear, yes! Yes. It was by the wind, Mr. Redlaw. By the wind.'

He had, by this time, put down the tray for dinner, and was employed in lighting the lamp, and spreading a cloth on the table. From this employment he desisted in a hurry, to stir and feed the fire, and then resumed it; the lamp he had lighted, and the blaze that rose under his hand, so quickly changing the appearance of the room, that it seemed as if the mere coming in of his fresh red face and active manner had made the pleasant alteration.

'Mrs. William is of course subject at any time, sir, to be taken off her balance by the elements. She is not formed superior to *that*.'

'No,' returned Mr. Redlaw good-naturedly, though abruptly.

'No, sir. Mrs. William may be taken off her balance by Earth; as, for example, last Sunday week, when sloppy and greasy, and she going out to tea with her newest sister-in-law, and having a pride in herself, and wishing to appear perfectly spotless, though pedestrian. Mrs. William may be taken off her balance by Air; as being once over-persuaded by a friend to try a swing at Peckham Fair, which acted on her constitution instantly like a steamboat. Mrs. William may be taken off her balance by Fire; as on a false alarm of engines at her mother's when she went two miles in her nightcap. Mrs. William may be taken off her balance by Water; as at Battersea, when rowed into the piers by her young nephew, Charley Swidger, junior, aged twelve, which had no idea of boats whatever. But these are elements. Mrs. William must be taken out of elements for the strength of *her* character to come into play.'

As he stopped for a reply, the reply was 'Yes,' in the same tone as before.

'Yes, sir. Oh dear, yes!' said Mr. Swidger, still proceeding with his preparations, and checking them off as he made them. 'That's where it is, sir. That's what I always say myself, sir. Such a many of us Swidgers! Pepper. Why, there's my father, sir, superannuated keeper and custodian of this Institution, eighty-seven years old. He's a Swidger! Spoon.'

'True, William,' was the patient and abstracted answer when he stopped again.

'Yes, sir,' said Mr. Swidger. 'That's what I always say, sir. You may call him the trunk of the tree! Bread. Then you come to his successor, my unworthy self – salt – and Mrs. William, Swidgers both. Knife and fork. Then you come to all my brothers and their families, Swidgers, man and woman, boy and girl. Why, what with cousins, uncles, aunts, and relationships of this, that, and t'other degree, and what-not degree, and marriages, and lyings-in, the Swidgers – tumbler – might take hold of hands, and make a ring round England!'

Receiving no reply at all here from the thoughtful man whom he addressed, Mr. William approached him nearer, and made a feint of accidentally knocking the table with a decanter to rouse him. The moment he succeeded, he went on, as if in great alacrity of aquiescence.

'Yes, sir! That's just what I say myself, sir. Mrs. William and me have often said so. "There's Swidgers enough," we say, "without *our* voluntary contributions." Butter. In fact, sir, my father is a family in himself – casters – to take care of; and it happens all for the best that we have no child of our own, though it's made Mrs. William rather quiet-like, too. Quite ready for the fowl and mashed potatoes, sir? Mrs. William said she'd dish in ten minutes when I left the Lodge.'

'I am quite ready,' said the other, waking as from a dream, and walking slowly to and fro.

'Mrs. William has been at it again, sir!' said the keeper, as he stood warming a plate at the fire, and pleasantly shading his face with it. Mr. Redlaw stopped in his walking, and an expression of intent appeared in him.

'What I always say myself, sir. She *will* do it! There's a motherly feeling in Mrs. William's breast that must and will have went.'

'What has she done?'

'Why, sir, not satisfied with being a sort of mother to all the young gentlemen that come up from a variety of parts, to attend your courses of lectures at this ancient foundation – It's surprising how stone-chaney catches the heat, this frosty weather, to be sure!' Here he turned the plates, and cooled his fingers.

'Well?' said Mr. Redlaw.

'That's just what I say myself, sir,' returned Mr. William, speaking over his shoulder, as if in ready and delighted assent. 'That's exactly where it is, sir! There ain't one of our students but appears to regard Mrs. William in that light. Every day, right through the course, they put their heads into the Lodge, one after another, and have all got something to tell her, or something to ask her. "Swidge" is the appellation by which they speak of Mrs. William in general, among themselves, I'm told; but that's what I say, sir. Better be called ever so far out of your name, if it's done in real liking, than have it made ever so much of, and not cared about! What's a name for? To know a person by. If Mrs. William is known by something better than her name – I allude to Mrs. William's qualities and disposition – never mind her name, though it *is* Swidger, by rights. Let 'em call her Swidge, Widge, Bridge – Lord!

London Bridge, Blackfriars, Chelsea, Putney, Waterloo, or Hammersmith Suspension – if they like!'

The close of this triumphant oration brought him and the plate to the table, upon which he half laid and half dropped it, with a lively sense of its being thoroughly heated, just as the subject of his praises entered the room, bearing another tray and a lantern, followed by a venerable old man with long grey hair.

Mrs. William, like Mr. William, was a simple innocent-looking person, in whose smooth cheeks the cheerful red of her husband's official waistcoat was very pleasantly repeated. But whereas Mr. William's light hair stood on end all over his head, and seemed to draw his eyes up with it in an excess of bustling readiness for anything, the dark brown hair of Mrs. William was carefully smoothed down, and waved away under a trim, tidy cap, in the most exact and quiet manner imaginable. Whereas Mr. William's very trousers hitched themselves up at the ankles, as if it were not in their iron-grey nature to rest without looking about them, Mrs. William's neatly-flowered skirts – red and white, like her own pretty face – were as composed and orderly as if the very wind that blew so hard out of doors could not disturb one of their folds. Whereas his coat had something of a fly-away and half-off appearance about the collar and breast, her little bodice was so placid and neat, that there should have been protection for her in it, had she needed any, with the roughest people. Who could have had the heart to make so calm a bosom swell with grief, or throb with fear, or flutter with a thought of shame? To whom would its repose and peace have not appealed against disturbance, like the innocent slumber of a child?

'Punctual, of course, Milly,' said her husband, relieving her of the tray, 'or it wouldn't be you. Here's Mrs. William, sir! He looks lonelier than ever tonight,' whispering to his wife as he was taking the tray, 'and ghostlier altogether.'

Without any show of hurry or noise, or any show of herself even, she was so calm and quiet, Milly set the dishes she had brought upon the table, Mr. William, after much clattering and running about, having only gained possession of a butter-boat of gravy, which he stood ready to serve.

'What is that the old man has in his arms?' asked Mr.

Redlaw as he sat down to his solitary meal.

'Holly, sir,' replied the quiet voice of Milly.

'That's what I say myself, sir,' interposed Mr. William, striking in with the butter-boat. 'Berries is so seasonable to the time of year! Brown gravy!'

'Another Christmas come, another year gone!' murmured the Chemist with a gloomy sigh. 'More figures in the lengthening sum of recollection that we work and work at to our torment, till Death idly jumbles all together, and rubs all out. So, Philip!' breaking off, and raising his voice as he addressed the old man standing apart, with his glistening burden in his arms, from which the quiet Mrs. William took small branches, which she noiselessly trimmed with his scissors, and decorated the room with, while her aged father-in-law looked on, much interested in the ceremony.

'My duty to you, sir,' returned the old man. 'Should have spoke before, sir, but know your ways, Mr. Redlaw – proud to say – and wait till spoke to! Merry Christmas, sir, and happy New Year, and many of 'em. Have had a pretty many of 'em myself – ha, ha! – and may take the liberty of wishing 'em. I'm eighty-seven!'

'Haven't you had so many that were merry and happy?' asked the other.

'Ay, sir, ever so many,' returned the old man.

'Is his memory impaired with age? It is to be expected now,' said Mr. Redlaw, turning to the son, and speaking lower.

'Not a morsel of it, sir,' replied Mr. William. 'That's exactly what I say myself, sir. There never was such a memory as my father's. He's the most wonderful man in the world. He don't know what forgetting means. It's the very observation I'm always making to Mrs. William, sir, if you'll believe me!'

Mr Swidger, in his polite desire to seem to acquiesce at all events, delivered this as if there were no iota of contradiction in it, and it were all said in unbounded and unqualified assent.

The Chemist pushed his plate away, and, rising from the table, walked across the room to where the old man stood looking at a little sprig of holly in his hand.

'It recalls the time when many of those years were old and new, then?' he said, observing him attentively, and touching him on the shoulder. 'Does it?'

'Oh, many, many!' said Philip, half awaking from his reverie. 'I'm eighty-seven!'

'Merry and happy, was it?' asked the Chemist in a low voice. 'Merry and happy, old man?'

'Maybe as high as that, no higher,' said the old man, holding out his hand a little way above the level of his knee, and looking retrospectively at his questioner, 'when I first remember 'em! Cold, sunshiny day it was, out a walking, when someone – it was my mother as sure as you stand there, though I don't know what her blessed face was like, for she took ill and died that Christmas-time – told me they were food for birds. The pretty little fellow thought – that's me, you understand – that birds' eyes were so bright, perhaps, because the berries that they lived on in the winter were so bright. I recollect that. And I'm eighty-seven!'

'Merry and happy!' mused the other, bending his dark eyes upon the stooping figure, with a smile of compassion. 'Merry and happy – and remember well?'

'Ay, ay, ay!' resumed the old man, catching the last words. 'I remember 'em well in my school-time, year after year, and all the merry-making that used to come along with them. I was a strong chap then, Mr. Redlaw; and, if you'll believe me, hadn't my match at football within ten mile. Where's my son William? Hadn't my match at football, William, within ten mile!'

'That's what I always say, father!' returned the son promptly, and with great respect. 'You *are* a Swidger, if ever there was one of the family!'

'Dear!' said the old man, shaking his head as he again looked at the holly. 'His mother – my son William's my youngest son – and I, have sat among 'em all, boys and girls, little children and babies, many a year, when the berries like these were not shining half so bright all round us, as their bright faces. Many of 'em are gone; she's gone; and my son George (our eldest, who was her pride more than all the rest) is fallen very low: but I can see them, when I look here, alive and healthy, as they used to be in those days; and I can see him, thank God, in his innocence. It's a blessed thing to me, at eighty-seven.'

The keen look that had been fixed upon him with so much earnestness had gradually sought the ground.

'When my circumstances got to be not so good as formerly, through not being honestly dealt by, and I first come here to be custodian,' said the old man, '– which was upwards of fifty years ago – where's my son William? More than half a century ago, William!'

'That's what I say, father,' replied the son as promptly and dutifully as before, 'that's exactly where it is. Two times ought's an ought, and twice five ten, and there's a hundred of 'em.'

'It was quite a pleasure to know that one of our founders – or, more correctly speaking,' said the old man, with a great glory in his subject and his knowledge of it, 'one of the learned gentlemen that helped endow us in Queen Elizabeth's time, for we were founded afore her day – left in his will, among the other bequests he made us, so much to buy holly, for garnishing the walls and windows come Christmas. There was something homely and friendly in it. Being but strange here then, and coming at Christmas-time, we took a liking for his very picter that hangs in what used to be, anciently, afore our ten poor gentlemen commuted for an annual stipend in money, our great Dinner Hall. A sedate gentleman in a peaked beard, with a ruff round his neck, and a scroll below him, in old English letters, "Lord, keep my memory green!" You know all about him, Mr. Redlaw?'

'I know the portrait hangs there, Philip.'

'Yes, sure, it's the second on the right, above the panelling. I was going to say – he has helped to keep *my* memory green, I thank him; for going round the building every year, as I'm a doing now, and freshening up the bare rooms with these branches and berries, freshens up my bare old brain. One year brings back another, and that year another, and those others numbers! At last, it seems to me as if the birth-time of our Lord was the birth-time of all I have ever had affection for, or mourned for, or delighted-in, and they're a pretty many, for I'm eighty-seven!'

'Merry and happy,' murmured Redlaw to himself.

The room began to darken strangely.

'So you see, sir,' pursued old Philip, whose hale, wintry cheek had warmed into a ruddier glow and whose blue eyes had brightened while he spoke, 'I have plenty to keep, when I keep this present season. Now, where's my quiet Mouse? Chattering's the sin of my time of life, and there's half the building to do yet, if the cold don't freeze us first, or the wind don't blow us away, or the darkness don't swallow us up.'

The quiet Mouse had brought her calm face to his side, and silently taken his arm, before he finished speaking.

'Come away, my dear,' said the old man. 'Mr. Redlaw won't settle to his dinner, otherwise, till it's cold as the winter. I hope you'll excuse me rambling on sir, and I wish you good night, and, once again, a merry —'

'Stay!' said Mr. Redlaw, resuming his place at the table, more, it would have seemed from his manner, to reassure the old keeper, than in any remembrance of his own appetite. 'Spare me another moment Philip. William, you were going to tell me something to your excellent wife's honour. It will not be disagreeable to her to hear you praise her. What was it?'

'Why, that's where it is, you see, sir,' returned Mr. William Swidger, looking towards his wife in considerable embarrassment. 'Mrs. William's got her eye upon me.'

'But you're not afraid of Mrs. William's eye?'

'Why, no, sir,' returned Mr. Swidger, 'that's what I say myself. It wasn't made to be afraid of. It wouldn't have been made so mild, if that was the intention. But I wouldn't like to – Milly! – him, you know. Down in the Buildings.'

Mr. William, standing behind the table, and rummaging disconcertedly among the objects upon it, directed persuasive glances at Mrs. William, and secret jerks of his head and thumb at Mr. Redlaw, as alluring her towards him.

'Him, you know, my love,' said Mr. William. 'Down in the Buildings. Tell, my dear! You're the works of Shakespeare in comparison with myself. Down in the Buildings, you know, my love. Student.'

'Student!' repeated Mr. Redlaw, raising his head.

'That's what I say, sir!' cried Mr. William in the utmost animation of assent. 'If it wasn't the poor student down in the Buildings, why should you wish to hear it from Mrs. William's lips? Mrs. William, my dear – Buildings.'

'I didn't know,' said Milly with a quiet frankness, free from any haste or confusion, 'that William had said anything about it, or I wouldn't have come. I asked him not to. It's a sick

young gentleman, sir – and very poor, I am afraid – who is too
ill to go home this holiday-time, and lives, unknown to any
one, in but a common kind of lodging for a gentleman, down
in Jerusalem Buildings. That's all, sir.'

'Why have I never heard of him?' said the Chemist, rising
hurriedly. 'Why has he not made his situation known to me?
Sick! Give me my hat and cloak. Poor! What house? – what
number?'

'Oh, you mustn't go there, sir!' said Milly, leaving her
father-in-law, and calmly confronting him with her collected
little face and folded hands.

'Not go there?'

'Oh dear, no!' said Milly, shaking her head as at a most
manifest and self-evident impossibility. 'It couldn't be thought
of!'

'What do you mean? Why not?'

'Why, you see, sir,' said Mr. William Swidger persuasively
and confidentially, 'that's what I say. Depend upon it, the
young gentleman would never have made his situation known
to one of his own sex. Mrs. William has got into his
confidence, but that's quite different. They all confide in Mrs.
William; they all trust *her*. A man, sir, couldn't have got a
whisper out of him; but woman, sir, and Mrs. William
combined —!'

'There is good sense and delicacy in what you say, William,'
returned Mr. Redlaw, observant of the gentle and composed
face at his shoulder. And laying his finger on his lip, he
secretly put his purse into her hand.

'Oh dear, no, sir!' cried Milly, giving it back again. 'Worse
and worse! Couldn't be dreamed of!'

Such a staid, matter-of-fact housewife she was, and so
unruffled by the momentary haste of this rejection, that, an
instant afterwards, she was tidily picking up a few leaves
which had strayed from between her scissors and her apron
when she had arranged the holly.

Finding, when she rose from her stooping posture, that Mr.
Redlaw was still regarding her with doubt and astonishment,
she quietly repeated – looking about, the while, for any other
fragments that might have escaped her observation:

'Oh dear, no, sir! He said that of all the world he would not be known to you, or receive help from you – though he is a student in your class. I have made no terms of secrecy with you, but I trust to your honour completely.'

'Why did he say so?'

'Indeed I can't tell, sir,' said Milly, after thinking a little, 'because I am not at all clever, you know; and I wanted to be useful to him in making things neat and comfortable about him, and employed myself that way. But I know he is poor and lonely, and I think he is somehow neglected too. How dark it is!'

The room had darkened more and more. There was a very heavy gloom and shadow gathering behind the Chemist's chair.

'What more about him?' he asked.

'He is engaged to be married when he can afford it,' said Milly, 'and is studying, I think, to qualify himself to earn a living. I have seen, a long time, that he has studied hard, and denied himself much. How very dark it is!'

'It's turned colder, too,' said the old man, rubbing his hands. 'There's a chill and dismal feeling in the room. Where's my son William? William, my boy, turn the lamp, and rouse the fire!'

Milly's voice resumed, like quiet music very softly played: 'He muttered in his broken sleep yesterday afternoon, after talking to me' (this as to herself), 'about someone dead, and some great wrong done that could never be forgotten; but whether to him or to another person, I don't know. Not *by* him, I am sure.'

'And, in short, Mrs. William, you see – which she wouldn't say herself, Mr. Redlaw, if she was to stop here till the new year after this next one,' said Mr. William, coming up to him to speak in his ear – 'has done him worlds of good! Bless you, worlds of good! All at home just the same as ever – my father made as snug and comfortable – not a crumb of litter to be found in the house, if you were to offer fifty pound ready money for it – Mrs. William apparently never out of the way – yet Mrs. William backwards and forwards, backwards and forwards, up and down, up and down, a mother to him!'

The room turned darker and colder, and the gloom and shadow gathering behind the chair was heavier.

'Not content with this, sir, Mrs. William goes and finds, this very night, when she was coming home (why, it's not above a couple of hours ago), a creature more like a young wild beast than a young child, shivering upon a doorstep. What does Mrs. William do, but brings it home to dry it, and feed it, and keep it till our old Bounty of food and flannel is given away on Christmas morning! If it ever felt a fire before, it's as much as it ever did; for it's sitting in the old Lodge chimney, staring at ours as if its ravenous eyes would never shut again. It's sitting there, at least,' said Mr. William, correcting himself, on reflection, 'unless it's bolted!'

'Heaven keep her happy!' said the Chemist aloud, 'and you too, Philip! and you, William! I must consider what to do in this. I may desire to see this student. I'll not detain you longer now. Good night!'

'I thankee, sir, I thankee!' said the old man, 'for Mouse, and for my son William, and for myself. Where's my son William? William, you take the lantern, and go on first, through them long dark passages, as you did last year and the year afore. Ha, ha! *I* remember – though I'm eighty-seven! "Lord, keep my memory green!" It's a very good prayer, Mr. Redlaw, that of the learned gentlemen in the peaked beard, with a ruff round his neck – hangs up, second on the right above the panelling, in what used to be, afore our ten poor gentleman commuted, our great Dinner Hall. "Lord, keep my memory green!" It's very good and pious, sir. Amen! Amen!'

As they passed out and shut the heavy door, which, however carefully withheld, fired a long train of thundering reverberations when it shut at last, the room turned darker.

As he fell a musing in his chair alone, the healthy holly withered on the wall, and dropped – dead branches.

As the gloom and shadow thickened behind him, in that place where it had been gathering so darkly, it took, by slow degrees, or out of it there came, by some unreal, unsubstantial process, not to be traced by any human sense, an awful likeness of himself.

Ghastly and cold, colourless in its leaden face and hands, but with his features, and his bright eyes, and his grizzled hair, and dressed in the gloomy shadow of his dress, it came into its terrible appearance of existence, motionless, without a sound.

As *he* leaned his arm upon the elbow of his chair, ruminating before the fire, *it* leaned upon the chair-back, close above him, with its appalling copy of his face looking where his face looked, and bearing the expression his face bore.

This, then, was the Something that had passed and gone already. This was the dead companion of the haunted man!

It took, for some moments, no more apparent heed of him than he of it. The Christmas Waits were playing somewhere in the distance, and, through his thoughtfulness, he seemed to listen to the music. It seemed to listen too.

At length he spoke; without moving or lifting up his face.

'Here again!' he said.

'Here again!' replied the Phantom.

'I see you in the fire,' said the haunted man. 'I hear you in music, in the wind, in the dead stillness of the night.'

The Phantom moved his head, assenting.

'Why do you come to haunt me thus?'

'I come as I am called,' replied the Ghost.

'No. Unbidden!' exclaimed the Chemist.

'Unbidden be it,' said the Spectre. 'It is enough. I am here.'

Hitherto the light of the fire had shone on the two faces – if the dread lineaments behind the chair might be called a face – both addressed towards it, as at first, and neither looking at the other. But, now, the haunted man turned suddenly, and stared upon the Ghost. The Ghost, as sudden in its motion, passed to before the chair, and stared on him.

The living man, and the animated image of himself dead, might so have looked, the one upon the other. An awful survey, in a lonely and remote part of an empty old pile of building, on a winter night, with the loud wind going by upon its journey of mystery – whence, or whither, no man knowing since the world began – and the stars, in unimaginable millions, glittering through it, from eternal space, where the world's bulk is as a grain, and its hoary age is infancy.

'Look upon me!' said the Spectre. 'I am he, neglected in my youth, and miserably poor, who strove and suffered, and still strove and suffered, until I hewed out knowledge from the mine where it was buried, and made rugged steps thereof, for my worn feet to rest and rest on.'

'I *am* that man,' returned the Chemist.

'No mother's self-denying love,' pursued the Phantom, 'no father's counsel, aided *me*. A stranger came into my father's place when I was but a child, and I was easily an alien from my mother's heart. My parents, at the best, were of that sort whose care soon ends, and whose duty is soon done; who cast their offspring loose early, as birds do theirs; and, if they do well, claim the merit; if ill, the pity.'

It paused, and seemed to tempt and goad him with its look, and with the manner of its speech, and with its smile.

'I am he,' pursued the Phantom, 'who, in this struggle upward, found a friend. I made him – won him – bound him to me! We worked together, side by side. All the love and confidence that in my ealier youth had had no outlet, and found no expression, I bestowed on him.'

'Not all,' said Redlaw hoarsely.

'No, not all,' returned the Phantom. 'I had a sister.'

The haunted man, with his head resting on his hands, replied, 'I had!' The Phantom, with an evil smile, drew closer to the chair, and resting its chin upon its folded hands, its folded hands upon the back, and looking down into his face with searching eyes, that seemed instinct with fire, went on:

'Such glimpses of the light of home as I had ever known, had streamed from her. How young she was, how fair, how loving! I took her to the first poor roof that I was master of, and made it rich. She came into the darkness of my life, and made it bright. She is before me!'

'I saw her, in the fire, but now. I hear her in music, in the wind, in the dead stillness of the night,' returned the haunted man.

'*Did* he love her?' said the Phantom, echoing his contemplative tone. 'I think he did once. I am sure he did. Better had she loved him less – less secretly, less dearly, from the shallower depths of a more divided hearth!'

'Let me forget it,' said the Chemist with an angry motion of his hand. 'Let me blot it from my memory!'

The Spectre, without stirring, and with its unwinking, cruel eyes still fixed upon his face, went on: 'A dream, like hers, stole upon my own life.'

'It did,' said Redlaw.

'A love, as like hers,' pursued the Phantom, 'as my inferior nature might cherish, arose in my own heart. I was too poor to bind its object to my fortune, then, by any thread of promise or entreaty. I loved her far too well to seek to do it. But, more than ever I had striven in my life, I strove to climb! Only an inch gained, brought me something nearer to the height. I toiled up! In the late pauses of my labour at that time – my sister (sweet companion!) still sharing with me the expiring embers and the cooling hearth – when day was breaking, what pictures of the future did I see!'

'I saw them in the fire but now,' he murmured. 'They come back to me in music, in the wind, in the dead stillness of the night, in the revolving years.'

'— Pictures of my own domestic life, in after-time, with her who was the inspiration of my toil. Pictures of my sister, made the wife of my dear friend, on equal terms – for he had some inheritance, we none – pictures of our sobered age and mellowed happiness, and of the golden links, extending back so far, that should bind us, and our children, in a radiant garland,' said the Phantom.

'Pictures,' said the haunted man, 'that were delusions. Why is it my doom to remember them too well?'

'Delusions,' echoed the Phantom in its changeless voice, and glaring on him with its changeless eyes. 'For my friend (in whose breast my confidence was locked as in my own), passing between me and the centre of the system of my hopes and struggles, won her to himself, and shattered my frail universe. My sister, doubly dear, doubly devoted, doubly cheerful in my home, lived on to see me famous, and my old ambition so rewarded when its spring was broken, and then —'

'Then died,' he interposed. 'Died, gentle as ever, happy, and with no concern but for her brother. Peace!'

The Phantom watched him silently.

'Remembered!' said the haunted man after a pause. 'Yes. So well remembered, that even now, when years have passed, and nothing is more idle or more visionary to me than the boyish love so long outlived, I think of it with sympathy, as if it were a younger brother's or a son's. Sometimes I even wonder when her heart first inclined to him, and how it had been affected towards me. Not lightly, once, I think. — But that is nothing. Early unhappiness, a wound from a hand I loved and trusted, and a loss that nothing can replace, outlive such fancies.'

'Thus,' said the Phantom, 'I bear within me a Sorrow and a Wrong. Thus I prey upon myself. Thus, memory is my curse; and, if I could forget my sorrow and my wrong, I would!'

'Mocker!' said the Chemist, leaping up, and making, with a wrathful hand, at the throat of his other self. 'Why have I always that taunt in my ears?'

'Forbear!' exclaimed the Spectre in an awful voice. 'Lay a hand on me, and die!'

He stopped midway, as if its words had paralysed him, and stood looking on it. It had glided from him; it had its arm raised high in warning; and a smile passed over its unearthly features as it reared its dark figure in triumph.

'If I could forget my sorrow and wrong, I would,' the Ghost repeated. 'If I could forget my sorrow and wrong, I would!'

'Evil spirit of myself,' returned the haunted man in a low, trembling tone, 'my life is darkened by that incessant whisper.'

'It is an echo,' said the Phantom.

'If it be an echo of my thoughts – as now, indeed, I know it is,' rejoined the haunted man, 'why should I, therefore, be tormented? It is not a selfish thought. I suffer it to range beyond myself. All men and women have their sorrows; most of them their wrongs; ingratitude, and sordid jealousy, and interest besetting all degrees of life. Who would not forget their sorrows and their wrongs?'

'Who would not, truly, and be the happier and better for it? said the Phantom.

'These revolutions of years, which we commemorate,' proceeded Redlaw, 'what do *they* recall? Are there any minds in which they do not re-awaken some sorrow, or some trouble? What is the remembrance of the old man who was here tonight? A tissue of sorrow and trouble.'

'But common natures,' said the Phantom, with its evil smile upon its glassy face, 'unenlightened minds and ordinary spirits, do not feel or reason on these things like men of higher cultivation and profounder thought.'

'Tempter,' answered Redlaw, 'whose hollow look and voice I dread more than words can express, and from whom some dim foreshadowing of greater fear is stealing over me while I speak, I hear again an echo of my own mind.'

'Receive it as a proof that I am powerful,' returned the Ghost. 'Hear what I offer! Forget the sorrow, wrong, and trouble you have known!'

'Forget them!' he repeated.

'I have the power to cancel their remembrance – to leave but very faint, confused traces of them, that will die out soon,' returned the Spectre. 'Say! Is it done?'

'Stay!' cried the haunted man, arresting by a terrified gesture the uplifted hand. 'I tremble with distrust and doubt of you; and the dim fear you cast upon me deepens into a nameless horror I can hardly bear. I would not deprive myself of any kindly recollection, or any sympathy that is good for me, or others. What shall I lose if I assent to this? What else will pass from my remembrance?'

'No knowledge; no result of study; nothing but the inter-twisted chain of feelings and associations; each in its turn dependent on, and nourished by, the banished recollections. Those will go.'

'Are they so many?' said the haunted man, reflecting in alarm.

'They have been wont to show themselves in the fire, in music, in the wind, in the dead stillness of the night, in the revolving years,' returned the Phantom scornfully.

'In nothing else?'

The Phantom held its peace.

But, having stood before him, silent, for a little while, it moved towards the fire; then stopped.

'Decide!' it said, 'before the opportunity is lost!'

'A moment! I call Heaven to witness,' said the agitated man, 'that I have never been a hater of my kind – never morose, indifferent, or hard to anything around me. If, living here alone, I have made too much of all that was and might have been, and too little of what is, the evil, I believe, has fallen on me, and not on others. But, if there were poison in my body, should I not, possessed of antidotes and knowledge how to use them, use them? If there be poison in my mind, and through this fearful shadow I can cast it out, shall I not cast it out?'

'Say,' said the Spectre, 'is it done?'

'A moment longer!' he answered hurriedly. '*I would forget it if I could*! Have *I* thought that alone, or has it been the thought of thousands upon thousands, generation after generation? All human memory is fraught with sorrow and trouble. My memory is as the memory of other men, but other men have not this choice. Yes, I close the bargain. Yes! I *will* forget my sorrow, wrong and trouble!'

'Say,' said the Spectre, 'is it done?'

'It is!'

'*It is*. And take this with you, man whom I here renounce! The gift that I have given, you shall give again, go where you will. Without recovering yourself the power that you have yielded up, you shall henceforth destroy its like in all whom you approach. Your wisdom has discovered that the memory of sorrow, wrong, and trouble is the lot of all mankind, and that mankind would be the happier, in its other memories, without it. Go! Be its benefactor! Freed from such remembrance, from this hour, carry involuntarily the blessing of such freedom with you. Its diffusion is inseparable and inalienable from you. Go! Be happy in the good you have won, and in the good you do!'

The Phantom, which had held its bloodless hand above him while it spoke, as if in some unholy invocation, or some ban; and which had gradually advanced its eyes so close to his, that he could see how they did not participate in the terrible smile upon its face, but were a fixed, unalterable, steady horror; melted from before him, and was gone.

As he stood rooted to the spot, possessed by fear and wonder, and imagining he heard repeated in melancholy echoes dying away fainter and fainter, the words, 'Destroy its like in all whom you approach!' a shrill cry reached his ears. It came, not from the passages beyond the door, but from another part of the old building, and sounded like the cry of someone in the dark who had lost the way.

He looked confusedly upon his hands and limbs, as if to be assured of his identity, and then shouted in reply, loudly and wildly; for there was a strangeness and terror upon him, as if he, too, were lost.

The cry responding, and being nearer, he caught up the lamp, and raised a heavy curtain in the wall, by which he was accustomed to pass into and out of the theatre where he lectured, which adjoined his room. Associated with youth and animation, and a high amphitheatre of faces which his entrance charmed to interest in a moment, it was a ghostly place when all this life was faded out of it, and stared upon him like an emblem of Death.

'Holloa!' he cried. 'Holloa! This way! Come to the light!' When, as he held the curtain with one hand, and with the other raised the lamp and tried to pierce the gloom that filled the place, something rushed past him into the room like a wild cat, and crouched down in a corner.

'What is it?' he said hastily.

He might have asked, 'What is it?' even had he seen it well, as presently he did when he stood looking at it gathered up in its corner.

A bundle of tatters, held together by a hand, in size and form almost an infant's, but in its greedy, desperate little clutch, a bad old man's. A face round and smoothed by some half-dozen years, but pinched and twisted by the experiences of a life. Bright eyes, but not youthful. Naked feet, beautiful in their childish delicacy, ugly in the blood and dirt that cracked upon them. A baby savage, a young monster, a child who had never been a child, a creature who might live to take the outward form of man, but who, within, would live and perish a mere beast.

Used, already, to be worried and hunted like a beast, the boy crouched down as he was looked at, and looked back again, and interposed his arm to ward off the expected blow.

'I'll bite,' he said, 'if you hit me!'

The time had been, and not many minutes since, when such a sight as this would have wrung the Chemist's heart. He looked upon it now coldly, but with a heavy effort to remember something – he did not know what – he asked the boy what he did there, and whence he came.

'Where's the woman?' he replied. 'I want to find the woman.'

'Who?'

'The woman. Her that brought me here, and set me by the

large fire. She was so long gone, that I went to look for her, and lost myself. I don't want you. I want the woman.'

He made a spring, so suddenly, to get away, that the dull sound of his naked feet upon the floor was near the curtain, when Redlaw caught him by his rags.

'Come! you let me go!' muttered the boy, struggling, and clenching his teeth. 'I've done nothing to you. Let me go, will you, to the woman?'

'That is not the way. There is a nearer one,' said Redlaw, detaining him, in the same blank effort to remember some association that ought of right to bear upon this monstrous object. 'What is your name?'

'Got none.'

'Where do you live?'

'Live! What's that?'

The boy shook his hair from his eyes to look at him for a moment, and then, twisting round his legs and wrestling with him, broke again into his repetition of, 'You let me go, will you? I want to find the woman.'

The Chemist led him to the door. 'This way,' he said, looking at him still confusedly, but with repugnance and avoidance, growing out of his coldness. 'I'll take you to her.'

The sharp eyes in the child's head, wandering round the room, lighted on the table where the remnants of the dinner were.

'Give me some of that!' he said covetously.

'Has she not fed you?'

'I shall be hungry again tomorrow, shan't I? Ain't I hungry every day?'

Finding himself released, he bounded at the table like some small animal of prey, and hugging to his breast bread and meat, and his own rags, all together, said:

'There! Now take me to the woman!'

As the Chemist, with a new-born dislike to touch him, sternly motioned him to follow, and was going out of the door, he trembled and stopped.

'The gift that I have given, you shall give again, go where you will.'

The Phantom's words were blowing in the wind, and the wind blew chill upon him.

'I'll not go there tonight,' he murmured faintly. 'I'll go nowhere tonight. Boy! straight down this long arched passage, and past the great dark door into the yard, you will see the fire shining on a window there.'

'The woman's fire?' inquired the boy.

He nodded, and the naked feet had sprung away. He came back with his lamp, locked his door hastily, and sat down in his chair, covering his face like one who was frightened at himself.

For now he was indeed alone. Alone, alone.

THE GIFT DIFFUSED

A small man sat in a small parlour, partitioned off from a small shop by a small screen, pasted all over with small scraps of newspapers. In company with the small man was almost any amount of small children you may please to name – at least, it seemed so; they made, in that very limited sphere of action, such an imposing effect, in point of numbers.

Of these small fry, two had, by some strong machinery, been got into bed in a corner, where they might have reposed snugly enough in the sleep of innocence, but for a constitutional propensity to keep awake, and also to scuffle in and out of bed. The immediate occasion of these predatory dashes at the waking world was the construction of an oyster-shell wall in a corner, by two other youths of tender age; on which fortification the two in bed made harassing descents (like those accursed Picts and Scots who beleaguer the early historical studies of most young Britons), and then withdrew to their own territory.

In addition to the stir attendant on these inroads, and the retorts of the invaded, who pursued hotly, and made lunges at the bedclothes, under which the marauders took refuge, another little boy, in another little bed, contributed his mite of confusion to the family stock, by casting his boots upon the waters; in other words, by launching these and several small objects, inoffensive in themselves, though of a hard substance considered as missiles, at the disturbers of his repose, who were not slow to return these compliments.

Besides which, another little boy – the biggest there, but still little – was tottering to and fro, bent on one side, and considerably affected in his knees by the weight of a large baby, which he was supposed, by a fiction that obtains sometimes in sanguine families, to be hushing to sleep. But oh! the inexhaustible regions of contemplation and watchfulness into which this baby's eyes were then only beginning to

27

compose themselves to stare over his unconscious shoulder!

It was a very Moloch of a baby, on whose insatiate altar the whole existence of this particular young brother was offered up a daily sacrifice. Its personality may be said to have consisted in its never being quiet, in any one place, for five consecutive minutes, and never going to sleep when required. 'Tetterby's baby' was as well known in the neighbourhood as the postman or the potboy. It roved from door-step to door-step, in the arms of little Johnny Tetterby, and lagged heavily at the rear of troops of juveniles who followed the Tumblers or the Monkey, and came up, all on one side, a little too late for everything that was attractive, from Monday morning until Saturday night. Wherever childhood congregated to play, there was little Moloch making Johnny fag and toil. Wherever Johnny desired to stay, little Moloch became fractious, and would not remain. Whenever Johnny wanted to go out, Moloch was asleep, and must be watched. Whenever Johnny wanted to stay at home, Moloch was awake, and must be taken out. Yet Johnny was verily persuaded that it was a faultless baby, without its peer in the realm of England; and was quite content to catch meek glimpses of things in general from behind its skirts, or over its limp flapping bonnet, and to go staggering about with it like a very little porter with a very large parcel, which was not directed to anybody, and could never be delivered anywhere.

The small man who sat in the small parlour, making fruitless attempts to read his newspaper peaceably in the midst of this disturbance, was the father of the family, and the chief of the firm described in the inscription over the little shop-front, by the name and title of A. TETTERBY AND CO., NEWSMEN. Indeed, strictly speaking, he was the only personage answering to that designation; as Co. was a merely poetical abstraction, altogether baseless and impersonal.

Tetterby's was the corner shop in Jerusalem Buildings. There was a good show of literature in the window, chiefly consisting of picture-newspapers out of date, and serial pirates and footpads. Walking-sticks, likewise, and marbles, were included in the stock-in-trade. It had once extended into the light confectionary line; but it would seem that those elegancies of life were not in demand about Jerusalem Buildings, for nothing connected with that branch of commerce remained in the window, except a sort of small glass lantern containing a languishing mass of bull's-eyes, which had melted in the summer and congealed in the winter, until all hope of ever getting them out, or of eating them without eating the lantern too, was gone for ever. Tetterby's had tried its hand at several things. It had once made a feeble little dart at the toy business; for, in another lantern, there was a heap of minute wax dolls, all sticking together upside down, in the direst confusion, with their feet on one another's heads and a precipitate of broken arms and legs at the bottom. It had made a move in the millinery direction, which a few dry, wiry bonnet-shapes remained in a corner of the window to attest. It had fancied that a living might lie hidden in the tobacco trade, and had stuck up a representation of a native of each of the three integral portions of the British empire in the act of consuming that fragrant weed; with a poetic legend attached, importing that united in one cause they sat and joked, one chewed tobacco, one took snuff, one smoked: but nothing seemed to have come of it – except flies. Time had been when it had put a forlorn trust in imitative jewellery, for in one pane of glass there was a card of cheap seals, and another of pencil-cases, and a mysterious black amulet of inscrutable intention labelled ninepence. But, to that hour, Jerusalem Buildings had bought none of them. In short, Tetterby's had tried so hard to get a livelihood out of Jerusalem Buildings in one way or other, and appeared to have done so indifferently in all, that the best position in the firm was too evidently Co.'s; Co., as a bodiless creation, being untroubled with the vulgar inconveniences of hunger and thirst, being chargeable neither to the poor's rates nor the assessed taxes, and having no family to provide for.

Tetterby himself, however, in his little palour, as already mentioned, having the presence of a young family impressed upon his mind in a manner too clamorous to be disregarded, or to comport with the quiet perusal of a newspaper, laid down his paper, wheeled, in his distraction, a few times round the parlour like an undecided carrier pigeon, made an ineffectual rush at one or two flying little figures in bedgowns that skimmed past him, and then, bearing suddenly down upon the only unoffending member of the family, boxed the ears of little Moloch's nurse.

'You bad boy!' said Mr. Tetterby; 'haven't you any feeling for your poor father after the fatigues and anxieties of a hard winter's day. Since five o'clock in the morning, but must you wither his rest, and corrode his latest intelligence, with *your* vicious tricks? Isn't it enough, sir, that your brother 'Dolphus is toiling and moiling in the fog and cold, and you rolling in the lap of luxury with a – with a baby, and everything you can wish for,' said Mr. Tetterby, heaping this up as a great climax of blessings, 'but must you make a wilderness of home, and maniacs of your parents? Must you, Johnny? Hey?' At each interrogation, Mr. Tetterby made a feint of boxing his ears again, but thought better of it, and held his hand.

'Oh, father!' whimpered Johnny, 'when I was'nt doing anything, I'm sure, but taking such care of Sally, and getting her to sleep. Oh, father!'

'I wish my little woman would come home!' said Mr. Tetterby, relenting and repenting; 'I only wish my little woman would come home! I ain't fit to deal with 'em. They make my head go round, and get the better of me. Oh, Johnny! Isn't it enough that your dear mother has provided you with that sweet sister!' indicating Moloch; 'isn't it enough that you were seven boys before, without a ray of gal, and that your dear mother went through what she *did* go through, on purpose that you might all of you have a little sister, but must you so behave yourself as to make my head swim?'

Softening more and more as his own tender feelings, and those of his injured son, were worked on, Mr. Tetterby concluded by embracing him, and immediately breaking away to catch one of the real delinquents. A reasonably good start occurring, he succeeded, after a short but smart run, and some rather severe cross-country work under and over the bed-steads, and in and out among the intricacies of the chairs, in capturing this infant, whom he condignly punished, and bore to bed. This example had a powerful, and apparently mesmer-ic, influence on him of the boots, who instantly fell into a deep sleep, though he had been, but a moment before, broad awake, and in the highest possible feather. Nor was it lost upon the two architects, who retired to bed, in an adjoining

closet, with great privacy and speed. The comrade of the
Intercepted One also shrinking into his nest with similar
discretion, Mr. Tetterby, when he paused for breath, found
himself unexpectedly in a scene of peace.

'My little woman herself,' said Mr. Tetterby, wiping his
flushed face, 'could hardly have done it better! I only wish my
little woman had had it to do, I do indeed!'

Mr. Tetterby sought upon his screen for a passage appropri-
ate to be impressed upon his children's minds on the occasion,
and read the following: '"It is an undoubted fact that all
remarkable men have had remarkable mothers, and have
respected them in after life as their best friends." Think of
your own remarkable mother, my boys,' said Mr. Tetterby,
'and know her value while she is still among you!'

He sat down again in his chair by the fire, and composed
himself, cross-legged, over his newspaper.

'Let anybody, I don't care who it is, get out of bed again,'
said Tetterby as a general proclamation, delivered in a very
soft-hearted manner, 'and astonishment will be the portion of
that respected contemporary!' – which expression Mr. Tetterby selected from his screen. 'Johnny, my child, take care of
your only sister, Sally; for she's the brightest gem that ever
sparkled on your early brow.'

Johnny sat down on a little stool, and devotedly crushed
himself beneath the weight of Moloch.

'Ah, what a gift that baby is to you, Johnny!' said his father;
'and how thankful you ought to be! "It is not generally
known," Johnny,' – was now referring to the screen again –
'"but it is a fact ascertained, by accurate calculations, that the
following immense percentage of babies never attain to two
years old; that is to say —"'

'Oh, don't, father, please!' cried Johnny. 'I can't bear it
when I think of Sally.'

Mr. Tetterby desisting, Johnny, with a profounder sense of
his trust, wiped his eyes, and hushed his sister.

'Your brother 'Dolphus,' said his father, poking the fire, 'is
late tonight, Johnny, and will come home like a lump of ice.
What's got your precious mother?'

'Here's mother, and 'Dolphus too, father,' exclaimed Johnny, 'I think!'

'You're right!' returned his father, listening. 'Yes, that's the footstep of my little woman.'

The process of induction, by which Mr. Tetterby had come to the conclusion that his wife was a little woman, was his own secret. She would have made two editions of himself very easily. Considered as an individual, she was rather remarkable for being robust and portly; but, considered with reference to her husband, her dimensions became magnificent. Nor did they assume a less imposing proportion when studied with reference to the size of her seven sons, who were but diminutive. In the case of Sally, however, Mrs. Tetterby had asserted herself at last; as nobody knew better than the victim Johnny, who weighed and measured that exacting idol every hour in the day.

Mrs. Tetterby, who had been marketing, and carried a basket, threw back her bonnet and shawl, and sitting down, fatigued, commanded Johnny to bring his sweet charge to her straightway for a kiss. Johnny having complied, and gone back to his stool, and again crushed himself, Master Adolphus Tetterby, who had by this time unwound his torso out of a prismatic comforter, apparently interminable, requested the same favour. Johnny having again complied, and again gone back to his stool, and again crushed himself, Mr. Tetterby, struck by a sudden thought, preferred the same claim on his own paternal part. The satisfaction of this third desire, completely exhausted the sacrifice, who had hardly breath enough left to get back to his stool, crush himself again, and pant at his relations.

'Whatever you do, Johnny,' said Mrs. Tetterby, shaking her head, 'take care of her, or never look your mother in the face again.'

'Nor your brother,' said Adolphus.

'Nor your father, Johnny,' added Mr. Tetterby.

Johnny, much affected by this conditional renunciation of him, looked down at Moloch's eyes to see that they were all right, so far, and skilfully patted her back (which was uppermost), and rocked her with his foot.

'Are you wet, 'Dolphus, my boy?' said his father. 'Come and take my chair, and dry yourself.'

'No, father, thankee,' said Adolphus, smoothing himself

down with his hands. 'I an't very wet, I don't think. Does my
face shine much, father?'

'Well, it *does* look waxy, my boy,' returned Mr. Tetterby.

'It's the weather, father,' said Adolphus, polishing his
cheeks on the worn sleeve of his jacket. 'What with rain, and
sleet, and wind, and snow, and fog, my face gets quite
brought out into a rash sometimes. And shines, it does – oh,
don't it, though!'

Master Adolphus was also in the newspaper line of life,
being employed, by a more thriving firm than his father and
Co., to vend newspapers at a railway station, where his
chubby little person, like a shabbily-disguised Cupid, and his
shrill little voice (he was not much more than ten years old),
were as well known as the hoarse panting of the locomotives
running in and out. His juvenility might have been at some
loss for a harmless outlet, in this early application to traffic,
but for a fortunate discovery he made of a means of entertain-
ing himself, and of dividing the long day into stages of
interest, without neglecting business. This ingenious inven-
tion, remarkable, like many great discoveries, for its simplic-
ity, consisted in varying the first vowel in the word 'paper,'
and substituting in its stead, at different periods of the day, all
the other vowels in grammatical succession. Thus, before
daylight in the winter-time, he went to and fro, in his little
oil-skin cap and cape, and his big comforter, piercing the
heavy air with his cry of 'Morn-ing Pa-per!' which, about an
hour before noon, changed to 'Morn-ing Pepper!' which, at
about two, changed to 'Morn-ing Pipper!' which, in a couple
of hours, changed to 'Morn-ing Pop-per!' and so declined
with the sun into 'Eve-ning Pup-per!' to the great relief and
comfort of this young gentleman's spirits.

Mrs. Tetterby, his lady mother, who had been sitting with
her bonnet and shawl thrown back, as aforesaid, thoughtfully
turning her wedding-ring round and round upon her finger,
now rose, and, divesting herself of her out-of-door attire,
began to lay the cloth for supper.

'Ah, dear me, dear me, dear me!' said Mrs. Tetterby.
'That's the way the world goes!'

'Which is the way the world goes, my dear?' asked Mr.
Tetterby, looking around.

'Oh, nothing!' said Mrs. Tetterby.

Mr. Tetterby elevated his eyebrows, folded his newspaper afresh, and carried his eyes up it, and down it, and across it, but was wandering in his attention, and not reading it.

Mrs. Tetterby, at the same time, laid the cloth, but rather as if she were punishing the table than preparing the family supper; hitting it unnecessarily hard with the knives and forks, slapping it with the plates, dinting it with the salt-cellar, and coming heavily down upon it with the loaf.

'Ah, dear me, dear me, dear me!' said Mrs. Tetterby. 'That's the way the world goes!'

'My duck,' returned her husband, looking round again, 'you said that before. Which is the way the world goes?'

'Oh, nothing!' said Mrs. Tetterby.

'Sophia!' remonstrated her husband, 'you said *that* before, too.'

'Well, I'll say it again if you like,' returned Mrs. Tetterby. 'Oh, nothing – there! And again if you like. Oh, nothing – there! And again if you like. Oh, nothing – now then!'

Mr. Tetterby brought his eye to bear upon the partner of his bosom, and said, in mild astonishment: 'My little woman what has put you out?'

'I'm sure *I* don't know,' she retorted. 'Don't ask me. Who said I was put out at all? *I* never did.'

Mr. Tetterby gave up the perusal of his newspaper as a bad job, and, taking a slow walk across the room, with his hands behind him, and his shoulders raised – his gait according perfectly with the resignation of his manner – addressed himself to his two eldest offspring.

'Your supper will be ready in a minute, 'Dolphus,' said Mr. Tetterby. 'Your mother has been out in the wet, to the cook's shop, to buy it. It was very good of your mother so to do. *You* shall get some supper too, very soon, Johnny. Your mother's pleased with you, my man, for being so attentive to your precious sister.'

Mrs. Tetterby, without any remark, but with a decided subsidence of her animosity towards the table, finished her preparations, and took from her ample basket a substantial slab of hot pease-pudding wrapped in paper, and a basin covered with a saucer, which, on being uncovered, sent forth an odour so agreeable, that the three pair of eyes in the two beds opened wide, and fixed themselves upon the banquet. Mr. Tetterby, without regarding this tacit invitation to be seated, stood repeating slowly, 'Yes, yes, your supper will be ready in a minute, 'Dolphus – your mother went out in the wet, to the cook's shop, to buy it. It was very good of your mother so to do' – until Mrs. Tetterby, who had been exhibiting sundry tokens of contrition behind him, caught him round the neck, and wept.

'Oh, 'Dolphus!' said Mrs. Tetterby, 'how could I go and behave so?'

This reconciliation affected Adolphus the younger and Johnny to that degree, that they both, as with one accord, raised a dismal cry, which had the effect of immediately shutting up the round eyes in the beds, and utterly routing the two remaining little Tetterbys, just then stealing in from the adjoining closet to see what was going on in the eating way.

'I am sure, 'Dolphus,' sobbed Mrs. Tetterby, 'coming home, I had no more idea than a child unborn —'

Mr. Tetterby seemed to dislike this figure of speech, and observed, 'Say than the baby, my dear.'

'— Had no more idea than the baby,' said Mrs. Tetterby. 'Johnny, don't look at me, but look at her, or she'll fall out of your lap and be killed, and then you'll die in agonies of a broken heart, and serve you right. No more idea, I hadn't than that darling, of being cross when I came home; but somehow 'Dolphus —' Mrs. Tetterby paused, and again turned her wedding-ring round and round upon her finger.

'I see!' said Mr. Tetterby. 'I understand! My little woman was put out. Hard times, and hard weather, and hard work, make it trying now and then. I see, bless your soul! No wonder! 'Dolf, my man,' continued Mr. Tetterby, exploring the basin with a fork, 'here's your mother been and bought, at the cook's shop, besides pease-pudding, a whole knuckle of a lovely roast leg of pork, with lots of crackling left upon it, and with seasoning, gravy, and mustard quite unlimited. Hand in your plate, my boy, and begin while it's simmering.'

Master Adolphus, needing no second summons, received his portion with eyes rendered moist by appetite, and, with-drawing to his particular stool, fell upon his supper tooth and nail. Johnny was not forgotten, but received his rations on bread, lest he should, in a flush of gravy, trickle any on the baby. He was required, for similar reasons, to keep his pudding, when not on active service, in his pocket.

There might have been more pork on the knuckle-bone – which knuckle-bone the carver at the cook's shop had assuredly not forgotten in carving for previous customers – but there was no stint of seasoning, and that is an accessory dreamily suggesting pork, and pleasantly cheating the sense of taste. The pease-pudding, too, the gravy and mustard, like the Eastern rose in respect of the nightingale, if they were not absolutely pork, had lived near it; so, upon the whole, there was the flavour of a middle-sized pig. It was irresistible to the Tetterbys in bed, who, though professing to slumber peacefully, crawled out when unseen by their parents, and silently appealed to their brothers for any gastronomic token of fraternal affection. They, not hard of heart, presenting scraps in return, it resulted that a party of light skirmishers in nightgowns were careering about the parlour all through supper, which harassed Mr. Tetterby exceedingly, and once or twice imposed upon him the necessity of a charge, before which these guerrilla troops retired in all directions, and in great confusion.

Mrs. Tetterby did not enjoy her supper. There seemed to be something on Mrs. Tetterby's mind. At one time she laughed without reason, and at another time she cried without reason, and at last she laughed and cried together in a manner so very unreasonable that her husband was confounded.

'My little woman,' said Mr. Tetterby, 'if the world goes that way, it appears to go the wrong way, and to choke you.'

'Give me a drop of water,' said Mrs. Tetterby, struggling with herself, 'and don't speak to me for the present, or take any notice of it. Don't do it!'

Mr. Tetterby, having administered the water, turned suddenly on the unlucky Johnny (who was full of sympathy), and demanded why he was wallowing there in gluttony and idleness, instead of coming forward with the baby, that the sight of her might revive his mother. Johnny immediately approached, borne down by its weight; but Mrs. Tetterby holding out her hand to signify that she was not in a condition to bear that trying appeal to her feelings, he was interdicted from advancing another inch, on pain of perpetual hatred from all his dearest connections; and accordingly retired to his stool again, and crushed himself as before.

After a pause Mrs. Tetterby said she was better now, and began to laugh.

'My little woman,' said her husband dubiously, 'are you quite sure you're better? Or are you, Sophia, about to break out in a fresh direction?'

'No, 'Dolphus, no,' replied his wife. 'I'm quite myself.' With that, settling her hair, and pressing the palms of her hands upon her eyes, she laughed again.

'What a wicked fool I was to think so for a moment!' said Mrs. Tetterby. 'Come nearer, 'Dolphus, and let me ease my mind, and tell you what I mean. Let me tell you all about it.'

Mr. Tetterby bringing his chair closer, Mrs. Tetterby laughed again, gave him a hug, and wiped her eyes.

'You know, 'Dolphus, my dear,' said Mrs. Tetterby, 'that when I was single, I might have given myself away in several directions. At one time, four after me at once; two of them were sons of Mars.'

'We're all sons of Ma's, my dear,' said Mr. Tetterby, 'jointly with Pa's.'

'I don't mean that,' replied his wife; 'I mean soldiers – sergeants.'

'Oh!' said Mr. Tetterby.

'Well, 'Dolphus, I'm sure I never think of such things now, to regret them; and I'm sure I've got as good a husband, and would do as much to prove that I was fond of him, as —'

'As any little woman in the world,' said Mr. Tetterby. 'Very good. *Very* good.'

If Mr. Tetterby had been ten feet high, he could not have expressed a gentler consideration for Mrs. Tetterby's fairy-like stature; and, if Mrs. Tetterby had been two feet high she could not have felt it more appropriately her due.

'But you see, 'Dolphus,' said Mrs. Tetterby, 'this being Christmas-time, when all people who can, make holiday, and when all people who have got money like to spend some, I did, somehow, get a little out of sorts when I was in the streets just now. There were so many things to be sold – such

delicious things to eat, such fine things to look at, such
delightful things to have – and there was so much calculating
and calculating necessary, before I durst lay out a sixpence for
the commonest thing; and the basket was so large, and wanted
so much in it; and my stock of money was so small, and
would go such a little way — You hate me, don't you,
'Dolphus?'

'Not quite,' said Mr. Tetterby, 'as yet.'

'Well! I'll tell you the whole truth' pursued his wife
penitently, 'and then perhaps you will. I felt all this so much,
when I was trudging about in the cold, and when I saw a lot of
other calculating faces and large baskets trudging about too,
that I began to think whether I mightn't have done better, and
been happier, if I hadn't —' The wedding-ring went round
again, and Mrs. Tetterby shook her downcast head as she
turned it.

'I see,' said her husband quietly; 'if you hadn't married at all,
or if you had married somebody else?'

'Yes,' sobbed Mrs. Tetterby. 'That's really what I thought.
Do you hate me now, 'Dolphus?'

'Why, no,' said Mr. Tetterby, 'I don't find that I do as yet.'

Mrs Tetterby gave him a thankful kiss, and went on.

'I begin to hope you won't, now, 'Dolphus, though I am
afraid I haven't told you the worst. I can't think what came
over me. I don't know whether I was ill, or mad, or what I
was, but I couldn't call up anything that seemed to bind us to
each other, or to reconcile me to my fortune. All the pleasures
and enjoyments we had ever had – *they* seemed so poor and
insignificant, I hated them. I could have trodden on them.
And I could think of nothing else except our being poor, and
the number of mouths there were at home.'

'Well, well, my dear,' said Mr. Tetterby, shaking her hand
encouragingly, 'that's truth, after all. We *are* poor, and there
are a number of mouths at home here.'

'Ah! but, Dolf, Dolf!' cried his wife, laying her hands upon
his neck, 'my good, kind, patient fellow, when I had been at
home a very little while – how different! Oh, Dolf dear, how
different it was! I felt as if there was a rush of recollection on
me, all at once, that softened my hard heart, and filled it up till
it was bursting. All our struggles for a livelihood, all our cares

and wants since we have been married, all the times of sickness, all the hours of watching, we have ever had, by one another, or by the children, seemed to speak to me, and say that they had made us one, and that I never might have been, or could have been, or would have been, any other than the wife and mother I am. Then the cheap enjoyments that I could have trodden on so cruelly, got to be so precious to me – oh, so priceless and dear! – that I couldn't bear to think how much I had wronged them; and I said, and say again a hundred times, how could I ever behave so, 'Dolphus? how could I ever have the heart to do it?'

The good woman, quite carried away by her honest tenderness and remorse, was weeping with all her heart, when she started up with a scream, and ran behind her husband. Her cry was so terrified, that the children started from their sleep and from their beds, and clung about her. Nor did her gaze belie her voice as she pointed to a pale man in a black cloak who had come into the room.

'Look at that man! Look there! What does he want?'

'My dear,' returned her husband, 'I'll ask him if you'll let me go. What's the matter? How you shake!'

'I saw him in the street when I was out just now. He looked at me, and stood near me. I am afraid of him.'

'Afraid of him! Why?'

'I don't know why – I – stop! husband!' for he was going towards the stranger.

She had one hand pressed upon her forehead, and one upon her breast; and there was a peculiar fluttering all over her, and a hurried unsteady motion of her eyes, as if she had lost something.

'Are you ill, my dear?'

'What is it that is going from me again?' she muttered in a low voice. 'What *is* this that is going away?'

Then she abruptly answered: 'Ill? No, I am quite well,' and stood looking vacantly at the floor.

Her husband, who had not been altogether free from the infection of her fear at first, and whom the present strangeness of her manner did not tend to reassure, addressed himself to the pale visitor in the black cloak, who stood still, and whose eyes were bent upon the ground.

'What may be your pleasure, sir,' he asked, 'with us?'

'I fear that my coming in unperceived,' returned the visitor, 'has alarmed you; but you were talking, and did not hear me.'

'My little woman says – perhaps you heard her say it,' returned Mr. Tetterby, 'that it's not the first time you have alarmed her tonight.'

'I am sorry for it. I remember to have observed her, for a few moments only, in the street. I had no intention of frightening her.'

As he raised his eyes in speaking, she raised hers. It was extraordinary to see what dread she had of him, and with what dread he observed it – and yet how narrowly and closely.

'My name,' he said, 'is Redlaw. I come from the old College hard by. A young gentleman, who is a student there, lodges in your house, does he not?'

'Mr Denham?' said Tetterby.

'Yes.'

It was a natural action, and so slight as to be hardly noticeable; but the little man, before speaking again, passed his hand across his forehead, and looked quickly round the room, as though he were sensible of some change in its atmosphere. The Chemist, instantly transferring to him the look of dread he had directed towards the wife, stepped back, and his face turned paler.

'The gentleman's room,' said Tetterby, 'is upstairs, sir. There's a more convenient private entrance; but, as you have come in here, it will save your going out into the cold, if you'll take this little staircase,' showing one communicating directly with the parlour, 'and go up to him that way, if you wish to see him.'

'Yes, I wish to see him,' said the Chemist. 'Can you spare a light?'

The watchfulness of his haggard look, and the inexplicable distrust that darkened it, seemed to trouble Mr. Tetterby. He paused; and, looking fixedly at him in return, stood for a minute or so, like a man stupefied or fascinated.

At length he said, 'I'll light you, sir, if you'll follow me.'

'No,' replied the Chemist, 'I don't wish to be attended, or announced to him. He does not expect me. I would rather go alone. Please to give me the light, if you can spare it, and I'll find the way.'

In the quickness of his expression of this desire, and in taking the candle from the newsman, he touched him on the breast. Withdrawing his hand hastily, almost as though he had wounded him by accident (for he did not know in what part of himself his new power resided, or how it was communicated, or how the manner of its reception varied in different persons), he turned and ascended the stair.

But, when he reached the top, he stopped and looked down. The wife was standing in the same place, twisting her ring round and round upon her finger. The husband, with his head bent forward on his breast, was musing heavily and sullenly. The children, still clustering about the mother, gazed timidly after the visitor, and nestled together when they saw him looking down.

'Come!' said the father roughly. 'There's enough of this. Get to bed here!'

'The place is inconvenient and small enough,' the mother added, 'without you. Get to bed!'

The whole brood, scared and sad, crept away: little Johnny and the baby lagging last. The mother glancing contemptuously round the sordid room, and tossing from her the fragments of her meal, stopped on the threshold of her task of clearing the table, and sat down, pondering idly and dejectedly. The father betook himself to the chimney-corner, and, impatiently raking the small fire together, bent over it as if he would monopolise it all. They did not interchange a word.

The Chemist, paler than before, stole upward like a thief; looking back upon the change below, and dreading equally to go on or return.

'What have I done?' he said confusedly. 'What am I going to do?'

'To be the benefactor of mankind,' he thought he heard a voice reply.

He looked round, but there was nothing there; and a passage now shutting out the little parlour from his view, he went on, directing his eyes before him at the way he went.

'It is only since last night,' he muttered gloomily, 'that I have remained shut up, and yet all things are strange to me. I am strange to myself. I am here as in a dream. What interest have I in this place, or in any place that I can bring to my remembrance? My mind is going blind!'

There was a door before him, and he knocked at it. Being invited, by a voice within, to enter, he complied.

'Is that my kind nurse?' said the voice. 'But I need not ask her. There was no one else to come here.'

It spoke cheerfully, though in a languid tone, and attracted his attention to a young man lying on a couch, drawn before the chimney-piece, with the back towards the door. A meagre, scanty stove, pinched and hollowed like a sick man's cheeks, and bricked into the centre of a hearth that it could scarcely warm, contained the fire, to which his face was turned. Being so near the windy housetop, it wasted quickly, and with a busy sound, and the burning ashes dropped down fast.

'They chink when they shoot out here,' said the student, smiling; 'so, according to the gossips, they are not coffins, but purses. I shall be well and rich yet, some day, if it please God, and shall live, perhaps, to love a daughter Milly, in remembrance of the kindest nature and the gentlest heart in the world.'

He put up his hand as if expecting her to take it, but, being weakened, he lay still, with his face resting on his other hand, and did not turn round.

The Chemist glanced about the room; at the student's books and papers, piled upon a table in a corner, where they, and his extinguished reading-lamp, now prohibited and put away, told of the attentive hours that had gone before this illness, and perhaps caused it; at such signs of his old health and freedom as the out-of-door attire that hung idle on the wall; at those remembrances of other and less solitary scenes, the little miniatures upon the chimney-piece, and the drawing of home; at that token of his emulation, perhaps, in some sort, of his personal attachment, too, the framed engraving of himself, the looker-on. The time had been, only yesterday, when not one of these objects, in its remotest association of interest with the living figure before him, would have been lost on Redlaw. Now, they were but objects; or, if any gleam of such connection shot upon him, it perplexed, and not enlightened him, as he stood looking round with a dull wonder.

The student, recalling the thin hand which had remained so

long untouched, raised himself on the couch, and turned his head.

'Mr **Redlaw**!' he exclaimed, and started up.

Redlaw **put** out his arm.

'Don't come near to me. I will sit here. Remain you where you are!'

He sat down on a chair near the door, and, having glanced at the young man standing leaning with his hand upon the couch, spoke with his eyes averted towards the ground.

'I heard, by an accident, by what accident is no matter, that one of my class was ill and solitary. I received no other description of him than that he lived in this street. Beginning my inquiries at the first house in it, I have found him.

'I have been ill, sir,' returned the student, not merely with a modest hesitation, but with a kind of awe of him, 'but am greatly better. An attack of fever – of the brain, I believe – has weakened me, but I am much better. I cannot say I have been solitary in my illness, or I should forget the ministering that has been near me.'

'You are speaking of the keeper's wife?' said Redlaw.

'Yes.' The student bent his head, as if he rendered her some silent homage.

The Chemist, in whom there was a cold, monotonous apathy, which rendered him more like a marble image on the tomb of the man who had started from his dinner yesterday at the first mention of this student's case, than the breathing man himself, glanced again at the student leaning with his hand upon the couch, and looked upon the ground, and in the air, as if for light for his blinded mind.

'I remembered your name,' he said, 'when it was mentioned to me downstairs just now; and I recollect your face. We have held but very little personal communication together?'

'Very little.'

'You have retired and withdrawn from me, more than any of the rest, I think?'

The student signified assent.

'And why?' said the Chemist; not with the least expression of interest, but with a moody, wayward kind of curiosity. 'Why? How comes it that you have sought to keep especially from me the knowledge of your remaining here, at this

season, when all the rest have dispersed, and of your being ill?
I want to know why this is?'

The young man, who had heard him with increasing
agitation, raised his downcast eyes to his face, and, clasping
his hands together, cried with sudden earnestness, and with
trembling lips:

'Mr. Redlaw! You have discovered me. You know my
secret!'

'Secret?' said the Chemist harshly. '*I* know?'

'Yes! Your manner, so different from the interest and
sympathy which endear you to so many hearts, your altered
voice, the constraint there is in everything you say, and in
your looks,' replied the student, 'warn me that you know me.
That you would conceal it, even now, is but a proof to me
(God knows I need none!) of your natural kindness, and of the
bar there is between us.'

A vacant and contemptuous laugh was all his answer.

'But Mr. Redlaw,' said the student, 'as a just man, and a
good man, think how innocent I am, except in name and
descent, of participation in any wrong inflicted on you, or in
any sorrow you have borne.'

'Sorrow!' said Redlaw, laughing. 'Wrong! What are those to
me?'

'For Heaven's sake,' entreated the shrinking student, 'do not
let the mere interchange of a few words with me change you
like this sir! Let me pass again from your knowledge and
notice. Let me occupy my old reserved and distant place
among those whom you instruct. Know me only by the name
I have assumed, and not by that of Langford —'

'Langford!' exclaimed the other.

He clasped his head with both his hands, and for a moment
turned upon the young man his own intelligent and thoughtful face. But the light passed from it like the sunbeam of an
instant, and it clouded as before.

'The name my mother bears, sir,' faltered the young man,
'the name she took, when she might, perhaps, have taken one
more honoured. Mr. Redlaw,' hesitating, 'I believe I know
that history. Where my infomation halts, my guesses at what
is wanting may supply something not remote from the truth. I
am the child of a marriage that has not proved itself a

well-assorted or a happy one. From infancy I have heard you spoken of with honour and respect – with something that was almost reverence. I have heard of such devotion, of such fortitude and tenderness, of such rising up against the obstacles which press men down, that my fancy, since I learnt my little lesson from my mother, has shed a lustre on your name. At last, a poor student myself, from whom could I learn but you?'

Redlaw, unmoved, unchanged, and looking at him with a staring frown, answered by no word or sign.

'I cannot say,' pursued the other, 'I should try in vain to say, how much it has impressed me, and affected me, to find the gracious traces of the past, in that certain power of winning gratitude and confidence which is associated among us students (among the humblest of us most) with Mr. Redlaw's generous name. Our ages and positions are so different, sir, and I am so accustomed to regard you from a distance, that I wonder at my own presumption when I touch, however lightly, on that theme. But to one who – I may say, who felt no common interest in my mother once – it may be something to hear, now that is all past, with what indescribable feelings of affection I have, in my obscurity, regarded him; with what pain and reluctance I have kept aloof from his encouragement, when a word of it would have made me rich; yet how I have felt it fit that I should hold my course, content to know him, and to be unknown. Mr. Redlaw,' said the student faintly, 'what I would have said, I have said ill, for my strength is strange to me as yet; but, for anything unworthy in this fraud of mine, forgive me, and for all the rest forget me!'

The staring frown remained on Redlaw's face, and yielded to no other expression until the student, with these words, advanced towards him, as if to touch his hand, when he drew back and cried to him:

'Don't come nearer to me!'

The young man stopped, shocked by the eagerness of his recoil, and by the sternness of his repulsion; and he passed his hand thoughtfully across his forehead.

'The past is past,' said the Chemist. 'It dies like the brutes. Who talks to me of its traces in my life? He raves or lies! What have I to do with your distempered dreams? If you want money, here it is. I came to offer it; and that is all I came for. There can be nothing else that brings me here,' he muttered, holding his head again with both his hands. 'There *can* be nothing else, and yet —'

He had tossed his purse upon the table. As he fell into this dim cogitation with himself, the student took it up, and held it out to him.

'Take it back, sir,' he said proudly, though not angrily. 'I wish you could take from me, with it, the remembrance of your words and offer.'

'You do?' he retorted, with a wild light in his eyes. 'You do?'

'I do!'

The Chemist went close to him for the first time, and took the purse, and turned him by the arm, and looked him in the face.

'There is sorrow and trouble in sickness, is there not?' he demanded with a laugh.

The wondering student answered, 'Yes.'

'In its unrest, in its anxiety, in its suspense, in all its train of physical and mental miseries?' said the Chemist with a wild, unearthly exultation. 'All best forgotten, are they not?'

The student did not answer, but again passed his hand confusedly across his forehead. Redlaw still held him by the sleeve, when Milly's voice was heard outside.

'I can see very well now,' she said, 'thank you, Dolf. Don't cry, dear. Father and mother will be comfortable again tomorrow, and home will be comfortable too. A gentleman with him, is there?'

Redlaw released his hold as he listened.

'I have feared, from the first moment,' he murmured to himself, 'to meet her. There is a steady quality of goodness in her that I dread to influence. I may be the murderer of what is tenderest and best within her bosom.'

She was knocking the door.

'Shall I dismiss it as an idle foreboding, or still avoid her?' he muttered, looking uneasily around.

She was knocking at the door again.

'Of all the visitors who could come here,' he said in a hoarse, alarmed voice, turning to his companion, 'this is the one I should desire most to avoid. Hide me!'

The student opened a frail door in the wall, communicating, where the garret roof began to slope towards the floor, with a small inner room. Redlaw passed in hastily, and shut it after him.

The student then resumed his place upon the couch, and called to her to enter.

'Dear Mr. Edmund,' said Milly, looking round, 'they told me there was a gentleman here.'

'There is no one here but I.'

'There has been someone?'

'Yes, yes, there has been someone.'

She put her little basket on the table, and went up to the back of the couch, as if to take the extended hand – but it was not there. A little surprised, in her quiet way, she leaned over to look at his face, and gently touching him on the brow.

'Are you quite as well tonight? Your head is not so cool as in the afternoon.'

'Tut!' said the student petulantly, 'very little ails me.'

A little more surprise, but no reproach, was expressed in her face, as she withdrew to the other side of the table, and took a small packet of needlework from her basket. But she laid it down again, on second thoughts, and going noiselessly about the room, set everything exactly in its place, and in the neatest order; even to the cushions on the couch, which she touched with so light a hand, that he hardly seemed to know it, as he lay looking at the fire. When all this was done, and she had swept the hearth, she sat down, in her modest little bonnet, to her work, and was quietly busy on it directly.

'It's the new muslin curtain for the window, Mr. Edmund,' said Milly, stitching away as she talked. 'It will look very clean and nice, though it costs very little, and will save your eyes, too, from the light. My William says the room should not be too light just now, when you are recovering so well, or the glare might make you giddy.'

He said nothing; but there was something so fretful and impatient in his change of position, that her quick fingers stopped, and she looked at him anxiously.

'The pillows are not comfortable,' she said, laying down her work and rising. 'I will soon put them right.'

'They were very well,' he answered. 'Leave them alone, pray. You make so much of everything.'

He raised his head to say this, and looked at her so thanklessly, that, after he had thrown himself down again, she stood timidly pausing. However, she resumed her seat, and her needle, without having directed even a murmuring look towards him, and was soon as busy as before.

'I have been thinking, Mr. Edmund, that *you* have been often thinking of late, when I have been sitting by, how true the saying is, that adversity is a good teacher. Health will be more precious to you, after this illness, than it has ever been. And years hence, when this time of year comes round, and you remember the days when you lay here sick, alone, that the knowledge of your illness might not afflict those who are dearest to you, your home will be doubly dear and doubly blessed. Now, isn't that a good, true thing?'

She was too intent upon her work, and too earnest in what she said, and too composed and quiet altogether, to be on the watch for any look he might direct towards her in reply; so the shaft of his ungrateful glance fell harmless, and did not wound her.

'Ah!' said Milly, with her pretty head inclining thoughtfully on one side, as she looked down, following her busy fingers with her eyes. 'Even on me – and I am very different from you, Mr. Edmund, for I have no learning, and don't know how to think properly – this view of such things has made a great impression since you have been lying ill. When I have seen you so touched by the kindness and attention of the poor people down-stairs, I have felt that you thought even that experience some repayment for the loss of health, and I have read in your face, as plain as if it was a book, that but for some trouble and sorrow we should never know half the good there is about us.'

His getting up from the couch interrupted her, or she was going on to say more.

'We needn't magnify the merit, Mrs. William,' he rejoined slightingly. 'The people downstairs will be paid in good time, I dare say, for any little extra service they may have rendered me; and perhaps they anticipate no less. I am much obliged to you, too.'

Her fingers stopped, and she looked at him.

'I can't be made to feel the more obliged by your exaggerating the case,' he said. 'I am sensible that you have been interested in me, and I say I am much obliged to you. What more would you have?'

Her work fell on her lap, as she still looked at him walking to and fro with an intolerant air, and stopping now and then.

'I say again, I am much obliged to you. Why weaken my sense of what is your due in obligation, by preferring enormous claims upon me? Trouble, sorrow, affliction, adversity! One might suppose I had been dying a score of deaths here.'

'Do you believe, Mr. Edmund,' she asked, rising and going nearer to him, 'that I spoke of the poor people of the house with any reference to myself? To me?' laying her hand upon her bosom with a simple and innocent smile of astonishment.

'Oh! I think nothing about it, my good creature,' he returned. 'I have had an indisposition, which your solicitude – observe! I say solicitude – makes a great deal more of than it merits; and it's over, and we can't perpetuate it.'

He coldly took a book, and sat down at the table.

She watched him for a little while, until her smile was quite gone, and then, returning to where her basket was, said gently:

'Mr. Edmund, would you rather be alone?'

'There is no reason why I should detain you here,' he replied.

'Except —' said Milly, hesitating, and showing her work.

'Oh! the curtain,' he answered with a supercilious laugh. 'That's not worth staying for.'

She made up the little packet again, and put it in her basket. Then, standing before him with such an air of patient entreaty that he could not choose but look at her, she said: 'If you should want me, I will come back willingly. When you did want me I was quite happy to come; there was no merit in it. I think you must be afraid that, now you are getting well, I may be troublesome to you; but I should not have been, indeed, I should have come no longer than your weakness and confinement lasted. You owe me nothing; but it is right that you should deal as justly by me as if I was a lady – even the very lady that you love; and, if you suspect me of meanly making

much of the little I have tried to do to comfort your
sick-room, you do yourself more wrong than ever you can do
me. That is why I am sorry. That is why I am very sorry.'

If she had been as passionate as she was quiet, as indignant as
she was calm, as angry in her look as she was gentle, as loud of
tone as she was low and clear, she might have left no sense of
her departure in the room, compared with that which fell
upon the lonely student when she went away.

He was gazing drearily upon the place where she had been,
when Redlaw came out of his concealment, and came to the
door.

'When sickness lays its hand on you again,' he said looking
fiercely back at him – 'may it be soon! – die here! Rot here!'

'What have you done?' returned the other catching at his
cloak. 'What change have you wrought in me? What curse
have you brought upon me? Give me back myself!'

'Give me back *myself*!' exclaimed Redlaw like a madman.
'I am infected. I am infectious! I am charged with poison for
my own mind, and the minds of all mankind. Where I
felt interest, compassion, sympathy, I am turning into
stone. Selfishness and ingratitude spring up in my blighting
footsteps. I am only so much less base than the wretches
whom I make so, that in the moment of their transforma-
tion I can hate them.'

As he spoke – the young man still holding to his cloak – he
cast him off, and struck him; then wildly hurried out into the
night air where the wind was blowing, the snow falling, the
cloud-drift sweeping on, the moon dimly shining; and where,
blowing in the wind, falling with the snow, drifting with the
clouds, shining in the moonlight, and heavily looming in the
darkness, were the Phantom's words, 'The gift that I have
given, you shall give again, go where you will!'

Whither he went he neither knew nor cared, so that he
avoided company. The change he felt within him made the
busy streets a desert, and himself a desert, and the multitude
around him, in their manifold endurances and ways of life, a
mighty waste of sand, which the winds tossed into unintelligi-
ble heaps, and made a ruinous confusion of. Those traces in his
breast which the Phantom had told him would 'die out soon'
were not, as yet, so far upon their way to death, but that he

understood enough of what he was, and what he made of others, to desire to be alone.

This put it in his mind – he suddenly bethought himself, as he was going along, of the boy who had rushed into his room. And then he recollected that, of those with whom he had communicated since the Phantom's disappearance, that boy alone had shown no sign of being changed.

Monstrous and odious as the wild thing was to him, he determined to seek it out, and prove if this were really so; and also to seek it with another intention, which came into his thoughts at the same time.

So, resolving with some difficulty where he was, he directed his steps back to the old College, and to that part of it where the general porch was, and where, alone, the pavement was worn by the tread of students' feet.

The keeper's house stood just within the iron gates, forming a part of the chief quadrangle. There was a little cloister outside, and from that sheltered place he knew he could look in at the window of their ordinary room, and see who was within. The iron gates were shut, but his hand was familir with the fastening, and, drawing it back by thrusting in his wrist between the bars, he passed through softly, shut it again, and crept up to the window, crumbling the thin crust of snow with his feet.

The fire, to which he had directed the boy last night, shining brightly through the glass, made an illuminated place upon the ground. Instinctively avoiding this, and going round it, he looked in at the window. At first he thought that there was no one there, and that the blaze was reddening only the old beams in the ceiling and the dark walls; but, peering in more narrowly, he saw the object of his search coiled asleep before it on the floor. He passed quickly to the door, opened it, and went in.

The creature lay in such a fiery heat, that, as the Chemist stooped to rouse him, it scorched his head. So soon as he was touched, the boy, not half awake, clutched his rags together with the instinct of flight upon him, half rolled and half ran into a distant corner of the room, where, heaped upon the ground, he stuck his foot out to defend himself.

'Get up!' said the Chemist. 'You have not forgotten me?'

'You let me alone!' returned the boy. 'This is the woman's house – not yours.'

The Chemist's steady eye controlled him somewhat, or inspired him with enough submission to be raised upon his feet, and looked at.

'Who washed them, and put those bandages where they were bruised and cracked?' asked the Chemist, pointing to their altered state.

'The woman did.'

'And is it she who has made you cleaner in the face, too?'

'Yes, the woman.'

Redlaw asked these questions to attract his eyes towards himself, and, with the same intent, now held him by the chin, and threw his wild hair back, though he loathed to touch him. The boy watched his eyes keenly, as if he thought it needful to his own defence, not knowing what he might do next; and Redlaw could see well that no change came over him.

'Where are they?' he inquired.

'The woman's out.'

'I know she is. Where is the old man with the white hair, and his son?'

'The woman's husband, d'ye mean?' inquired the boy.

'Ay. Where are those two?'

'Out. Something's the matter somewhere. They were fetched out in a hurry, and told me to stop here.'

'Come with me,' said the Chemist, 'and I'll give you money.'

'Come where? and how much will you give?'

'I'll give you more shillings than you ever saw, and bring you back soon. Do you know your way to where you came from?'

'You let me go,' returned the boy, suddenly twisting out of his grasp. 'I'm not a-going to take you there. Let me be, or I'll heave some fire at you!'

He was down before it, and ready, and with his savage little hand, to pluck the burning coals out.

What the Chemist had felt, in observing the effect of his charmed influence stealing over those with whom he came in contact, was not nearly equal to the cold vague terror with which he saw this baby-monster put in at defiance. It chilled his blood to look on the immovable, impenetrable thing, in the likeness of a child, with its sharp malignant face turned up to his, and its almost infant hand ready at the bars.

'Listen, boy!' he said. 'You shall take me where you please, so that you take me where the peole are very miserable or very wicked. I want to do them good, and not to harm them. You shall have money, as I have told you, and I will bring you back. Get up! Come quickly!' He made a hasty step towards the door, afraid of her returning.

'Will you let me walk by myself, and never hold me, nor yet touch me?' said the boy, slowly withdrawing the hand with which he threatened, and beginning to get up.

'And let me go before, behind, or anyways I like?'

'I will!'

'Give me some money first, then, and I'll go.'

The Chemist laid a few shillings, one by one, in his extended hand. To count them was beyond the boy's knowledge, but he said, 'one,' every time, and avariciously looked at each as it was given, and at the donor. He had nowhere to put them, out of his hand, but in his mouth; and he put them there.

Redlaw then wrote with his pencil, on a leaf of his pocketbook, that the boy was with him; and, laying it on the table, signed to him to follow. Keeping his rags together, as usual, the boy complied, and went out with his bare head and his naked feet into the winter night.

Preferring not to depart by the iron gate by which he had entered, where they were in danger of meeting her whom he so anxiously avoided, the Chemist led the way, through some of those passages among which the boy had lost himself, and by that portion of the building where he lived, to a small door of which he had the key. When they got into the street, he stopped to ask his guide – who instantly retreated from him – if he knew where they were.

The savage thing looked here and there, and at length, nodding his head, pointed in the direction he designed to take. Redlaw going on at once, he followed, somewhat less suspiciously; shifting his money from his mouth into his hand, and back again into his mouth, and stealthily rubbing it bright upon his shreds of dress, as he went along.

Three times, in their progress, they were side by side. Three times they stopped, being side by side. Three times the Chemist glanced down at his face, and shuddered as it forced upon him one reflection.

The first occasion was when they were crossing an old churchyard, and Redlaw stopped among the graves, utterly at a loss how to connect them with any tender, softening, or consolatory thought.

The second was when the breaking forth of the moon induced him to look up at the heavens, where he saw her in her glory, surrounded by a host of stars he still knew by the names and histories which human science has appended to them; but where he saw nothing else he had been wont to see, felt nothing he had been wont to feel, in looking up there on a bright night.

The third was when he stopped to listen to a plaintive strain of music, but could only hear a tune, made manifest to him by the dry mechanism of the instruments and his own ears, with no address to any mystery within him, without a whisper in it of the past, or of the future, powerless upon him as the sound of last year's running water, or the rushing of last year's wind.

At each of these three times he saw, with horror, that in spite of the vast intellectual distance between them, and their being unlike each other in all physical respects, the expression on the boy's face was the expression on his own.

They journeyed on for some time – now through such crowded places, that he often looked over his shoulder, thinking he had lost his guide, but generally finding him within his shadow on his other side; now by ways so quiet, that he could have counted his short, quick, naked footsteps coming on behind – until they arrived at a ruinous collection of houses, and the boy touched him and stopped.

'In there!' he said, pointing out one house where there were scattered lights in the windows, and a dim lantern in the doorway, with 'Lodgings for Travellers' painted on it.

Redlaw looked about him; from the houses, to the waste piece of ground on which the houses stood, or rather, did not altogether tumble down, unfenced, undrained, unlighted, and bordered by a sluggish ditch; from that, to the sloping line of arches, part of some neighbouring viaduct or bridge with which it was surrounded, and which lessened gradually towards them, until the last but one was a mere kennel for a dog, the last a plundered little heap of brick; from that, to the child, close to him, cowering and trembling with the cold, and limping on one little foot, while he coiled the other round his leg to warm it, yet staring at all these things with that frightful likeness of expression so apparent in his face, that Redlaw started from him.

'In there!' said the boy, pointing out the house again. 'I'll wait.'

'Will they let me in?' asked Redlaw.

'Say you're a doctor,' he answered with a nod. 'There's plenty ill here.'

Looking back on his way to the house-door, Redlaw saw him trail himself upon the dust, and crawl within the shelter of the smallest arch, as if he were a rat. He had no pity for the thing, but he was afraid of it; and when it looked out of its den at him, he hurried to the house as a retreat.

'Sorrow, wrong, and trouble,' said the Chemist, with a painful effort at some more distinct remembrance, 'at least haunt this place darkly. He can do no harm who brings forgetfulness of such things here!'

With these words he pushed the yielding door, and went in.

There was a woman sitting on the stairs, either asleep or forlorn, whose head was bent down on her hands and knees. As it was not easy to pass without treading on her, and as she was perfectly regardless of his near approach, he stopped, and touched her on the shoulder. Looking up, she showed him quite a young face, but one whose bloom and promise were all swept away, as if the haggard winter should unnaturally kill the spring.

With little or no show of concern on his account, she moved nearer to the wall to leave him a wider passage.

'What are you?' said Redlaw, pausing, with his hand upon the broken stair-rail.

'What do you think I am?' she answered, showing him her face again.

He looked upon the ruined temple of God, so lately made, so soon disfigured; and something, which was not compassion – for the springs in which a true compassion for such miseries has its rise were dried up in his breast – but which was nearer to it, for the moment, than any feeling that had lately struggled into the darkening, but not yet wholly darkened, night of his mind – mingled a touch of softness with his next words.

'I am come here to give relief, if I can,' he said. 'Are you thinking of any wrong?'

She frowned at him, and then laughed; and then her laugh prolonged itself into a shivering sigh, as she dropped her head again, and hid her fingers in her hair.

'Are you thinking of a wrong?' he asked once more.

'I am thinking of my life,' she said with a momentary look at him.

He had a perception that she was one of many, and that he saw the type of thousands when he saw her drooping at his feet.

'What are your parents?' he demanded.

'I had a good home once. My father was a gardener, far away into the country.'

'Is he dead?'

'He's dead to me. All such things are dead to me. You a gentleman, and not know that!' She raised her eyes again, and laughed at him.

'Girl!' said Redlaw sternly, 'before this death of all such things was brought about, was there no wrong done to you? In spite of all that you can do, does no remembrance of wrong cleave to you? Are there not times upon times when it is misery to you?'

So little of what was womanly was left in her appearance, that now, when she burst into tears, he stood amazed. But he was more amazed, and much disquieted, to note, in her awakened recollection of this wrong, the first trace of her old humanity and frozen tenderness appeared to show itself.

He drew a little off, and, in doing so, observed that her arms were black, her fact cut, and her bosom bruised.

'What brutal hand has hurt you so?' he asked.

'My own. I did it myself!' she answered quickly.

'It is impossible.'

'I'll swear I did! He didn't touch me. I did it to myself in a passion, and threw myself down here. He wasn't near me. He never laid a hand upon me!'

In the white determination of her face, confronting him with this untruth, he saw enough of the last perversion and distortion of good surviving in that miserable breast, to be stricken with remorse that he had ever come near here.

'Sorrow, wrong, and trouble!' he muttered, turning his fearful gaze away. 'All that connects her with the state from which she has fallen has those roots! In the name of God, let me go by!'

Afraid to look at her again, afraid to touch her, afraid to think of having sundered the last thread by which she held upon the mercy of Heaven, he gathered his cloak about him, and glided swiftly up the stairs.

Opposite to him, on the landing, was a door, which stood partly open, and which, as he ascended, a man with a candle in his hand came forward from within to shut. But this man, on seeing him, drew back, with much emotion in his manner, and, as if by a sudden impulse, mentioned his name aloud.

In the surprise of such a recognition there, he stopped, endeavouring to recollect the wan and startled face. He had no time to consider it, for, to his yet greater amazement, old Philip came out of the room, and took him by the hand.

'Mr Redlaw,' said the old man, 'this is like you, this is like you, sir! You have heard of it, and have come after us to render any help you can. Ah, too late, too late!'

Redlaw, with a bewildered look, submitted to be led into the room. A man lay there on a truckle-bed, and William Swidger stood at the bedside.

'Too late!' murmured the old man, looking wistfully into the Chemist's face; and the tears stole down his cheeks.

'That's what I say, father,' interposed his son in a low voice. 'That's where it is exactly. To keep as quiet as ever we can while he's dozing is the only thing to do. You're right, father!'

Redlaw paused at the bedside, and looked down on the figure that was stretched upon the mattress. It was that of a man who should have been in the vigour of his life, but on whom it was not likely that the sun would ever shine again. The vices of his forty or fifty years' career had so branded him, that, in comparison with their effects upon his face, the heavy hand of time upon the old man's face who watched him had been merciful and beautifying.

'Who is this?' asked the Chemist, looking round.

'My son George, Mr. Redlaw,' said the old man, wringing his hands. 'My eldest son, George, who was more his mother's pride than all the rest!'

Redlaw's eyes wandered from the old man's grey head, as he laid it down upon the bed, to the person who had recognised him, and who had kept aloof in the remotest corner of the room. He seemed to be about his own age; and, although he knew no such hopeless decayed and broken man as he appeared to be, there was something in the turn of his figure, as he stood with his back towards him, and now went out at the door, that made him pass his hand uneasily across his brow.

'William,' he said in a gloomy whisper, 'who is that man?'

'Why, you see, sir,' returned Mr. William, 'that's what I say myself. Why should a man ever go and gamble, and the like of that, and let himself down inch by inch till he can't let himself down any lower?'

'Has *he* done so?' asked Redlaw, glancing after him with the same uneasy action as before.

'Just exactly that, sir,' returned William Swidger, 'as I'm told. He knows a little about medicine, sir, it seems; and having been wayfaring towards London with my unhappy brother that you see here,' – Mr. William passed his coatsleeve across his eyes – 'and being lodging upstairs for the night – what I say, you see, is, that strange companions come together here sometimes – he looked in to attend upon him, and came for us at his request. What a mournful spectacle, sir! But that's where it is. It's enough to kill my father!'

Redlaw looked up at these words, and, recalling where he was and with whom, and the spell he carried with him – which his surprise had obscured – retired a little, hurriedly, debating with himself whether to shun the house that moment, or remain.

Yielding to a certain sullen doggedness, which it seemed to be part of his condition to struggle with, he argued for remaining.

'Was it only yesterday,' he said, 'when I observed the

memory of this old man to be a tissue of sorrow and trouble, and shall I be afraid, tonight, to shake it? Are such remembrances as I can drive away so precious to this dying man, that I need fear for *him*? No, I'll stay here.'

But he stayed in fear and trembling none the less for these words; and, shrouded in his black cloak with his face turned from them, stood away from the bedside, listening to what they said, as if he felt himself a demon in the place.

'Father!' murmured the sick man, rallying a little from his stupor.

'My boy! My son George!' said old Philip.

'You spoke, just now, of my being mother's favourite long ago. It's a dreadful thing to think, now, of long ago!'

'No, no, no!' returned the old man. 'Think of it. Don't say it's dreadful. It's not dreadful to me, my son.'

'It cuts you to the heart, father.' For the old man's tears were falling on him.

'Yes, yes,' said Philip, 'so it does; but it does me good. It's a heavy sorrow to think of that time, but it does me good, George. Oh, think of it too, think of it too, and your heart will be softened more and more! Where's my son William? William, my boy, your mother loved him dearly to the last, and with her latest breath said, "Tell him I forgave him, blessed him, and prayed for him." Those were her words to me. I have never forgotten them, and I'm eighty-seven!'

'Father!' said the man upon the bed, 'I am dying, I know. I am so far gone, that I can hardly speak, even of what my mind most runs on. Is there any hope for me beyond this bed?'

'There is hope,' returned the old man, 'for all who are softened and penitent. There is hope for all such. Oh!' he exclaimed, clasping his hands and looking up, 'I was thankful, only yesterday, that I could remember this unhappy son when he was an innocent child. But what a comfort is it, now, to think that even God himself has that remembrance of him!'

Redlaw spread his hands upon his face, and shrunk like a murderer.

'Ah!' feebly moaned the man upon the bed. 'The waste since then, the waste of life since then!'

'But he was a child once,' said the old man. 'He played with children. Before he lay down on his bed at night, and fell into his guiltless rest, he said his prayers at his poor mother's knee. I have seen him do it many a time; and seen her lay his head upon her breast and kiss him. Sorrowful as it was to her, and to me, to think of this, when he went so wrong, and when our hopes and plans for him were all broken, this gave him still a hold upon us, that nothing else could have given. Oh, Father, so much better than the fathers upon earth! Oh, Father, so much more afflicted by the errors of thy children! take this wanderer back! Not as he is, but as he was then, let him cry to thee, as he has so often seemed to cry to us!'

As the old man lifted up his trembling hands, the son, for whom he made the supplication, laid his sinking head against him for support and comfort, as if he were indeed the child of whom he spoke.

When did man ever tremble as Redlaw trembled in the silence that ensued? He knew it must come upon them, knew that it was coming fast.

'My time is very short, my breath is shorter,' said the sick man, supporting himself on one arm, and with the other groping in the air, 'and I remember there is something on my mind concerning the man who was here just now. Father and William – wait! – is there really anything in black out there?'

'Yes, yes, it is real,' said his aged father.

'Is it a man?'

'What I say myself George,' interposed his brother, bending kindly over him. 'It's Mr. Redlaw.'

'I thought I had dreamed of him. Ask him to come here.'

The Chemist, whiter than the dying man, appeared before him. Obedient to the motion of his hand, he sat upon the bed.

'It has been so ripped up tonight, sir,' said the sick man, laying his hand upon his heart, with a look in which the mute, imploring agony of his condition was concentrated, 'by the sight of my poor old father, and the thought of all the trouble I have been the cause of, and all the wrong and sorrow lying at my door that —'

Was it the extremity to which he had come, or was it the dawning of another change, that made him stop?

'— that what I *can* do right, with my mind running on so much, so fast, I'll try to do. There was another man here. Did you see him?'

Redlaw could not reply by any word; for when he saw that fatal sign he knew so well now, of the wandering hand upon the forehead, his voice died at his lips. But he made some indication of assent.

'He is penniless, hungry, and destitute. He is completely beaten down, and has no resource at all. Look after him! Lose no time! I know he has it in his mind to kill himself.'

It was working. It was on his face. His face was changing, hardening, deepening in all its shades, and losing all its sorrow.

'Don't you remember? Don't you know him?' he pursued.

He shut his face out for a moment with the hand that again wandered over his forehead and then it lowered on Redlaw, reckless, ruffianly, and callous.

'Why, d—n you!' he said, scowling round, 'what have you been doing to me here? I have lived bold, and I mean to die bold. To the Devil with you!'

And so he lay down upon his bed, and put his arms up over his head and ears, as resolute from that time to keep out all access, and to die in his indifference.

If Redlaw had been struck by lightning, it could not have struck him from the bedside with a more tremendous shock. But the old man, who had left the bed while his son was speaking to him, now returning, avoided it quickly likewise, and with abhorrence.

'Where's my boy William?' said the old man hurriedly. 'William, come away from here. We'll go home.'

'Home, father!' returned William. 'Are you going to leave your own son?'

'Where's my own son?' replied the old man.

'Where? Why, there!'

'That's no son of mine,' said Philip, trembling with resentment. 'No such wretch as that has any claim on me. My children are pleasant to look at, and they wait upon me, and get my meat and drink ready, and are useful to me. I've a right to it! I'm eighty-seven!'

'You're old enough to be no older,' muttered William, looking at him grudgingly, with his hands in his pockets. 'I don't know what good you are myself. We could have a deal more pleasure without you.'

'*My* son, Mr. Redlaw!' said the old man. '*My* son, too! The boy talking to me of *my* son! Why, what has he ever done to give me any pleasure, I should like to know?'

'I don't know what you have ever done to give *me* any pleasure,' said William sulkily.

'Let me think,' said the old man. 'For how many Christmas-times running have I sat in my warm place, and never had to come out in the cold night air; and have made good cheer, without being disturbed by any such uncomfortable, wretched sight as him there? Is it twenty, William?'

'Nigh forty, it seems,' he muttered. 'Why, when I look at my father, sir, and come to think of it,' addressing Redlaw with an impatience and an irritation that were quite new, 'I'm whipped if I can see anything in him but a calendar of ever so many years of eating, and drinking, and making himself comfortable over and over again.'

'I – I'm eighty-seven,' said the old man, rambling on, childishly and weakly, 'and I don't know as I ever was much put out by anything. I'm not-a-going to begin now, because of what he calls my son. He's not my son. I've had a power of pleasant times. I recollect once – no, I don't – no, it's broken off. It was something about a game of cricket and a friend of mine, but it's somehow broken off. I wonder who he was – I suppose I liked him? And I wonder what became of him – I suppose he died? But I don't know. And I don't care, neither; I don't care a bit.'

In his drowsy chuckling, and the shaking of his head, he put his hands into his waistcoat pockets. In one of them he found a bit of holly (left there, probably, last night), which he now took out, and looked at.

'Berries, eh?' said the old man. 'Ah! It's a pity they're not good to eat. I recollect when I was a little chap about as high as that, and out a walking with – let me see – who was I out a walking with? – no, I don't remember how that was. I don't remember as I ever walked with any one particular, or cared for any one, or any one for me. Berries, eh? There's good cheer when there's berries. Well, I ought to have my share of it, and to be waited on, and kept warm and comfortable; for I'm eighty-seven, and a poor old man. I'm eighty-seven. Eighty-seven!'

The drivelling, pitiable manner in which, as he repeated this, he nibbled at the leaves, and spat the morsels out; the cold, uninterested eye with which his youngest son (so changed) regarded him; the determined apathy with which his eldest son lay hardened in his sin; impressed themselves no more on Redlaw's observation; for he broke his way from the spot to which his feet seemed to have been fixed, and ran out of the house.

His guide came crawling forth from his place of refuge, and was ready for him before he reached the arches.

'Back to the woman's?' he inquired.

'Back quickly!' answered Redlaw. 'Stop nowhere on the way!'

For a short distance the boy went on before; but their return was more like a flight than a walk, and it was as much as his bare feet could do to keep pace with the Chemist's rapid strides. Shrinking from all who passed, shrouded in his cloak, and keeping it drawn closely about him, as though there were mortal contagion in any fluttering touch of his garments, he made no pause until they reached the door by which they had come out. He unlocked it with his key, went in, accompanied by the boy, and hastened through the dark passages to his own chamber.

The boy watched him as he made the door fast, and withdrew behind the table when he looked round.

'Come!' he said. 'Don't you touch me! You've not brought me here to take my money away.'

Redlaw threw some more upon the ground. He flung his body on it immediately, as if to hide it from him, less the sight of it should tempt him to reclaim it; and not until he saw him seated by his lamp, with his face hidden in his hands, began furtively to pick it up. When he had done so, he crept near the fire, and, sitting down in a great chair before it, took from his breast some broken scraps of food, and fell to munching, and to staring at the blaze, and now and then to glancing at his shillings, which he kept clenched up in a bunch in one hand.

'And this,' said Redlaw, gazing on him with increasing repugnance and fear, 'is the only one companion I have left on earth!'

How long it was before he was aroused from his contemplation of this creature whom he dreaded so – whether half an hour, or half the night – he knew not. But the stillness of the room was broken by the boy (whom he had seen listening) starting up, and running towards the door.

'Here's the woman coming!' he exclaimed.

The Chemist stopped him on his way, at the moment when she knocked.

'Let me go to her, will you?' said the boy.

'Not now,' returned the Chemist. 'Stay here. Nobody must pass in or out of the room now. Who's that?'

'It's I, sir,' cried Milly. 'Pray, sir, let me in.'

'No! not for the world!' he said.

'Mr. Redlaw, Mr. Redlaw, pray, sir, let me in!'

'What is the matter?' he said, holding the boy.

'The miserable man you saw is worse, and nothing I can say will wake him from his terrible infatuation. William's father has turned childish in a moment. William himself is changed. The shock has been too sudden for him; I cannot understand him: he is not like himself. Oh, Mr. Redlaw, pray advise me, help me!'

'No! No! No!' he answered.

'Mr. Redlaw! Dear sir! George has been muttering in his doze about the man you saw there, who, he fears, will kill himself.'

'Better he should do it than come near me!'

'He says, in his wandering, that you know him; that he was your friend once, long ago; that he is the ruined father of a student here – my mind misgives me, of the young gentleman who has been ill. What is to be done? How is he to be followed? How is he to be saved? Mr. Redlaw, pray, oh, pray advise me! Help me!'

All this time he held the boy, who was half mad to pass him, and let her in.

'Phantoms! Punishers of impious thoughts!' cried Redlaw, gazing round in anguish. 'Look upon me! From the darkness of my mind, let the glimmering of contrition that I know is there, shine up and show my misery! In the material world, as I have long taught, nothing can be spared; no step or atom in the wondrous structure could be lost, without a blank being made in the great universe. I know, now, that it is the same with good and evil, happiness and sorrow, in the memories of men. Pity me! Relieve me!'

There was no response but her 'Help me, help me, let me in!' and the boy's struggling to get to her.

'Shadow of myself! Spirit of my darker hours!' cried Redlaw in distraction. 'Come back, and haunt me day and night, but take this gift away! Or, if it must still rest with me, deprive me of the dreadful power of giving it to others. Undo what I had done. Leave me benighted, but restore the day to those whom I have cursed. As I have spared this woman from the first, and as I never will go forth again, but will die here, with no hand to tend me, save this creature's who is proof against me – hear me!'

The only reply still was, the boy struggling to get to her, while he held him back; and the cry increasing in its energy, 'Help! let me in! He was your friend once: how shall he be followed, how shall he be saved? They are all changed, there is no one else to help me: pray, pray let me in!'

THE GIFT REVERSED

Night was still heavy in the sky. On open plains, from hill-tops, and from the decks of solitary ships at sea, a distant low-lying line, that promised by-and-by to change to light, was visible in the dim horizon; but its promise was remote and doubtful, and the moon was striving with the night clouds busily.

The shadows upon Redlaw's mind succeeded thick and fast to one another, and obscured its light as the night clouds hovered between the moon and earth, and kept the latter veiled in darkness. Fitful and uncertain as the shadows which the night clouds cast were their concealments from him, and imperfect revelations to him; and, like the night clouds still, if the clear light broke forth for a moment, it was only that they might sweep over it, and make the darkness deeper than before.

Without, there was a profound and solemn hush upon the ancient pile of building, and its buttresses and angles made dark shapes of mystery upon the ground, which now seemed to retire into the smooth white snow, and now seemed to come out of it, as the moon's path was more or less beset. Within, the Chemist's room was indistinct and murky, by the light of the expiring lamp; a ghostly silence had succeeded to the knocking and the voice outside; nothing was audible but, now and then, a low sound among the whitened ashes of the fire, as of its yielding up its last breath. Before it, on the ground, the boy lay fast asleep. In his chair the Chemist sat, as he had sat there since the calling at his door had ceased – like a man turned to stone.

At such a time the Christmas music he had heard before began to play. He listened to it, at first, as he had listened in the churchyard; but presently – it playing still, and being borne towards him on the night air, in a low, sweet melancholy strain – he rose, and stood stretching his hands about him, as if there were some friend approaching within his reach, on

66

whom his desolate touch might rest, yet do no harm. As he did this, his face became less fixed and wondering; a gentle trembling came upon him; and at last his eyes filled with tears, and he put his hands before them, and bowed down his head.

His memory of sorrow, wrong, and trouble had not come back to him; he knew that it was not restored; he had no passing belief or hope that it was. But some dumb stir within him made him capable, again, of being moved by what was hidden, afar off, in the music. If it were only that it told him sorrowfully the value of what he had lost, he thanked Heaven for it with a fervent gratitude.

As the last chord died upon his ear, he raised his head to listen to its lingering vibration. Beyond the boy, so that his sleeping figure lay at its feet, the Phantom stood, immovable and silent, with its eyes upon him.

Ghastly it was, as it had ever been, but not so cruel and relentless in its aspect – or he thought or hoped so, as he looked upon it, trembling. It was not alone, but in its shadowy hand it held another hand.

And whose was that? Was the form that stood beside it indeed Milly's, òr but her shade and picture? The quiet head was bent a little, as her manner was and her eyes were looking down, as if in pity, on the sleeping child. A radiant light fell on her face, but did not touch the Phantom; for, though close beside her, it was dark and colourless as ever.

'Spectre!' said the Chemist, newly troubled as he looked, 'I have not been stubborn or presumptuous in respect of her. Oh, do not bring her here! Spare me that!'

'This is but a shadow,' said the Phantom; 'when the morning shines, seek out the reality whose image I present before you.'

'Is it my inexorable doom to do so?' cried the Chemist.

'It is,' replied the Phantom.

'To destroy her peace, her goodness; to make her what I am myself, and what I have made of others?'

'I have said, "Seek her out,"' returned the Phantom. 'I have said no more.'

'Oh, tell me!' exclaimed Redlaw, catching at the hope which he fancied might lie hidden in the words. 'Can I undo what I have done?'

'No,' returned the Phantom.

'I do not ask for restoration to myself,' said Redlaw. 'What I abandoned, I abandoned of my own will, and have justly lost. But for those to whom I have transferred the fatal gift; who never sought it; who unknowingly received a curse of which they had no warning, and which they had no power to shun; can I do nothing?'

'Nothing,' said the Phantom.

'If I cannot, can anyone?'

The Phantom, standing like a statue, kept its gaze upon him for awhile; then turned its head suddenly, and looked upon the shadow at its side.

'Ah! Can she?' cried Redlaw, still looking upon the shade.

The Phantom released the hand it had retained till now, and softly raised its own with a gesture of dismissal. Upon that, her shadow, still preserving the same attitude, began to move or melt away.

'Stay!' cried Redlaw with an earnestness to which he could not give enough expression. 'For a moment! As an act of mercy! I know that some change fell upon me when those sounds were in the air just now. Tell me, have I lost the power of harming her? May I go near her without dread? Oh, let her give me any sign of hope!'

The Phantom looked upon the shade as he did – not at him – and gave no answer.

'At least, say this – has she, henceforth, the consciousness of any power to set right what I have done?'

'She has not,' the Phantom answered.

'Has she the power bestowed on her without the consciousness?'

The Phantom answered: 'Seek her out.' And her shadow slowly vanished.

They were face to face again, and looking on each other as intently and awfully as at the time of the bestowal of the gift, across the boy who still lay on the ground between them, at the Phantom's feet.

'Terrible instructor,' said the Chemist, sinking on his knee before it in an attitude of supplication, 'by whom I was renounced, but by whom I am revisited (in which, and in whose milder aspect, I would fain believe I have a gleam of hope), I will obey without inquiry, praying that the cry I have sent up in the anguish of my soul has been, or will be, heard on behalf of those whom I have injured beyond human reparation. But there is one thing –'

'You speak to me of what is lying here, the Phantom interposed, and pointed with its finger to the boy.

'I do,' returned the Chemist. 'You know what I would ask. Why has this child alone been proof against my influence, and why, why have I detected in its thoughts a terrible companionship with mine?'

'This,' said the Phantom, pointing to the boy, 'is the last, completest illustration of a human creature utterly bereft of such remembrances as you have yielded up. No softening memory of sorrow, wrong, or trouble enters here, because this wretched mortal from his birth has been abandoned to a worse condition than the beasts, and has, within his knowledge, no one contrast, no humanising touch to make a grain of such a memory spring up in his hardened breast. All within this desolate creature is barren wilderness. All within the man bereft of what you have resigned is the same barren wilderness. Woe to such a man! Woe, tenfold, to the nation that shall count its monsters such as this, lying here by hundreds and by thousands!'

Redlaw shrunk, appalled, from what he heard.

'There is not,' said the Phantom, 'one of these – not one – but sows a harvest that mankind *must* reap. From every seed of evil in this boy a field of ruin is grown that shall be gathered in, and garnered up, and sown again in many places in the world, until regions are overspread with wickedness enough to raise the waters of another Deluge. Open and unpunished murder in a city's streets would be less guilty in its daily toleration than one such spectacle as this.'

It seemed to look down upon the boy in his sleep. Redlaw, too, looked down upon him with a new emotion.

'There is not a father,' said the Phantom, 'by whose side, in his daily or his nightly walk, these creatures pass; there is not a mother among all the ranks of loving mothers in this land; there is no one risen from the state of childhood, but shall be responsible in his or her degree for this enormity. There is not a country throughout the earth on which it would not bring a curse. There is no religion upon earth that it would not deny; there is no people upon earth it would not put to shame.'

The Chemist clasped his hands, and looked, with trembling fear and pity, from the sleeping boy to the Phantom, standing above him with its finger pointing down.

'Behold, I say,' pursued the Spectre, 'the perfect type of what it was your choice to be. Your influence is powerless here, because from this child's bosom you can banish nothing. His thoughts have been in "terrible companionship" with yours, because you have gone down to his unnatural level. He is the growth of man's indifference; you are the growth of man's presumption. The beneficent design of Heaven is, in each case, overthrown, and from the two poles of the immaterial world you come together.'

The Chemist stooped upon the ground beside the boy, and, with the same kind of compassion for him that he now felt for himself, covered him as he slept, and no longer shrunk from him with abhorrence or indifference.

Soon, now, the distant line on the horizon brightened, the darkness faded, the sun rose red and glorious, and the chimney-stacks and gables of the ancient building gleamed in the clear air, which turned the smoke and vapour of the city into a cloud of gold. The very sun-dial in his shady corner, where the wind was used to spin with such unwindy constancy, shook off the finer particles of snow that had accumulated on his dull old face in the night, and looked out at the little white wreaths eddying round and round him. Doubtless some blind groping of the morning made its way down into the forgotten crypt, so cold and earthy, where the Norman arches were half buried in the ground, and stirred the dull sap in the lazy vegetation hanging to the walls, and quickened the slow principle of life within the little world of wonderful and delicate creation which existed there, with some faint knowledge that the sun was up.

The Tetterbys were up, and doing. Mr. Tetterby took down the shutters of the shop, and, strip by strip, revealed the treasures of the window to the eyes, so proof against their seductions, of Jerusalem Buildings. Adolphus had been out so long already, that he was half-way on to Morning Pepper. Five small Tetterbys, whose ten round eyes were much

inflamed by soap and friction, were in the tortures of a cool
wash in the back-kitchen; Mrs. Tetterby presiding. Johnny,
who was pushed and hustled through his toilet with great
rapidity when Moloch chanced to be in an exacting frame of
mind (which was always the case), staggered up and down
with his charge before the shop-door, under greater difficulties than usual; the weight of Moloch being much increased by
a complication of defences against the cold, composed of
knitted worsted-work, and forming a complete suit of chain-
armour, with a head-piece and blue gaiters.

It was a peculiarity of this baby to be always cutting teeth.
Whether they never came, or whether they came and went
away again, is not in evidence; but it had certainly cut enough,
on the showing of Mrs. Tetterby, to make a handsome dental
provision for the sign of the Bull and Mouth. All sorts of
objects were impressed for the rubbing of its gums, notwithstanding that it always carried, dangling at its waist (which
was immediately under its chin), a bone ring, large enough to
have represented the rosary of a young nun. Knife handles,
umbrella tops, the heads of walking-sticks selected from the
stock, the fingers of the family in general, but especially of
Johnny, nutmeg-graters, crusts, the handles of doors, and the
cook knobs on the tops of pokers, were among the commonest instruments indiscriminately applied for this baby's
relief. The amount of electricity that must have been rubbed
out of it in a week is not to be calculated. Still Mrs. Tetterby
always said 'it was coming through, and then the child would
be herself;' and still it never did come through, and the child
continued to be somebody else.

The tempers of the little Tetterbys had sadly changed with a
few hours. Mr. and Mrs. Tetterby themselves were not more
altered than their offspring. Usually they were an unselfish,
good-natured, yielding little race, sharing short commons
when it happened (which was pretty often) contentedly, and
even generously, and taking a great deal of enjoyment out of a
very little meat. But they were fighting now, not only for the
soap-and-water, but even for the breakfast which was yet in
perspective. The hand of every little Tetterby was against the
other little Tetterbys; and even Johnny's hand – the patient,
much-enduring, and devoted Johnny – rose against the baby!

Yes. Mrs. Tetterby, going to the door by a mere accident, saw him viciously pick out a weak place in the suit of armour, where a slap would tell, and slap that blessed child.

Mrs. Tetterby had him into the parlour, by the collar, in that same flash of time, and repaid him the assault with usury thereto.

'You brute, you murdering little boy!' said Mrs. Tetterby. 'Had you the heart to do it?'

'Why don't her teeth come through, then,' retorted Johnny in a loud rebellious voice, 'instead of bothering me? How would you like it yourself?'

'Like it, sir!' said Mrs. Tetterby, relieving him of his dishonoured load.

'Yes, like it,' said Johnny. 'How would you? Not at all. If you was me, you'd go for a soldier. I will, too. There an't no babies in the army.'

Mr. Tetterby, who had arrived upon the scene of action, rubbed his chin thoughtfully, instead of correcting the rebel, and seemed rather struck by this view of a military life.

'I wish I was in the army myself, if the child's in the right,' said Mrs. Tetterby, looking at her husband, 'for I have no peace in my life here. I'm a slave – a Virginia slave,' some indistinct association with their weak descent on the tobacco trade, perhaps, suggested this aggravated expression to Mrs. Tetterby. 'I never have a holiday, or any pleasure at all, from year's end to year's end! Why, Lord bless and save the child,' said Mrs. Tetterby, shaking the baby with an irritability hardly suited to so pious an aspiration, 'what's the matter with her now?'

Not being able to discover, and not rendering the subject much clearer by shaking it, Mrs. Tetterby put the baby away in a cradle, and, folding her arms, sat rocking it angrily with her foot.

'How you stand there, 'Dolphus!' said Mrs. Tetterby to her husband. 'Why don't you do something?'

'Because I don't care about anything,' Mr. Tetterby replied.

'I'm sure I don't,' said Mrs. Tetterby.

'I'll take my oath I don't,' said Mr. Tetterby.

A diversion arose here among Johnny and his five younger brothers, who, in preparing the family breakfast-table, had fallen to skirmishing for the temporary possession of the loaf, and were buffering one another with great heartiness; the smallest boy of all, with precocious discretion, hovering outside the knot of combatants, and harassing their legs. Into the midst of this fray Mr. and Mr. Tetterby both precipitated themselves with great ardour, as if such ground were the only ground on which they could now agree; and having, with no visible remains of their late soft-heartedness, laid about them without any lenity, and done much execution, resumed their former relative positions.

'You had better read your paper than do nothing at all,' said Mrs. Tetterby.

'What's there to read in a paper?' returned Mr. Tetterby with excessive discontent.

'What?' said Mrs. Tetterby. 'Police.'

'It's nothing to me,' said Tetterby. 'What do I care what people do, or are done to?'

'Suicides,' suggested Mrs. Tetterby.

'No business of mine,' replied her husband.

'Births, deaths, and marriages, are those nothing to you?' said Mrs. Tetterby.

'If the births were all over for good and all today; and the deaths were all to begin to come off tomorrow; I don't see why it should interest me, till I thought it was a-coming to my turn,' grumbled Tetterby. 'As to marriages, I've done it myself. I know quite enough about *them*.'

To judge from the dissatisfied expression of her face and manner, Mrs. Tetterby appeared to entertain the same opinions as her husband; but she opposed him, nevertheless, for the gratification of quarrelling with him.

'Oh! you're a consistent man,' said Mrs. Tetterby, 'an't you? You, with the screen of your own making there, made of nothing else but bits of newspapers, which you sit and read to the children by the half-hour together!'

'Say used to, if you please,' returned her husband. 'You won't find me doing so any more. I'm wiser now.'

'Bah! Wiser, indeed!' said Mrs. Tetterby. 'Are you better?'

The question sounded some discordant note in Mr. Tetterby's breast. He ruminated dejectedly, and passed his hand across and across his forehead.

'Better!' murmured Mr. Tetterby. 'I don't know as any of us are better, or happier either. Better is it?'

He turned to the screen, and traced about it with his finger, until he found a certain paragraph of which he was in quest.

'This used to be one of the family favourites, I recollect,' said Tetterby in a forlorn and stupid way, 'and used to draw tears from the children, and make 'em good, if there was any little bickering or discontent among 'em, next to the story of the robin redbreasts in the wood. "Melancholy case of destitution. Yesterday a small man, with a baby in his arms, and surrounded by half-a-dozen ragged little ones, of various ages between ten and two, the whole of whom were evidently in a famishing condition, appeared before the worthy magistrate, and made the following recital." Ha! I don't understand it, I'm sure,' said Tetterby; 'I don't see what it has got to do with us.'

'How old and shabby he looks!' said Mrs. Tetterby, watching him. 'I never saw such a change in a man. Ah! dear me, dear me, dear me, it was a sacrifice!'

'What was a sacrifice?' her husband sourly inquired.

Mrs. Tetterby shook her head; and, without replying in words, raised a complete sea-storm about the baby by her violent agitation of the cradle.

'If you mean your marriage was a sacrifice, my good woman –' said her husband.

'I *do* mean it,' said his wife.

'Why, then, I mean to say,' pursued Mr. Tetterby as sulkily and surlily as she, 'that there are two sides to that affair; and that *I* was the sacrifice; and that I wish the sacrifice hadn't been accepted.'

'I wish it hadn't, Tetterby, with all my heart and soul, I do assure you,' said his wife. 'You can't wish it more than I do, Tetterby.'

'I don't know what I saw in her,' muttered the newsman, 'I'm sure; certainly, if I saw anything, it's not there now. I was thinking so last night, after supper, by the fire. She's fat, she's ageing, she won't bear comparison with most other women.'

'He's common-looking, he has no air with him, he's small, he's beginning to stoop, and he's getting bald,' muttered Mrs. Tetterby.

'I must have been half out of my mind when I did it,' muttered Mr. Tetterby.

'My senses must have forsook me. That's the only way in which I can explain it to myself,' said Mrs. Tetterby with elaboration.

In this mood they sat down to breakfast. The little Tetterbys were not habituated to regard that meal in the light of a sedentary occupation, but discussed it as a dance or trot; rather resembling a savage ceremony, in the occasional shrill whoops and brandishings of bread-and-butter with which it was accompanied, as well as in the intricate filings off into the street and back again, and the hoppings up and down the doorsteps, which were incidental to the performance. In the present instance, the contentions between these Tetterby children for the milk-and-water jug, common to all, which stood upon the table, presented so lamentable an instance of angry passions risen very high indeed, that it was an outrage on the memory of Doctor Watts. It was not until Mr. Tetterby had driven the whole herd out of the front-door that a moment's peace was secured; and even that was broken by the discovery that Johnny had surreptitiously come back, and was at that instant choking in the jug like a ventriloquist, in his indecent and rapacious haste.

'These children will be the death of me at last!' said Mrs. Tetterby after banishing the culprit. 'And the sooner the better I think.'

'Poor people,' said Mr. Tetterby, 'ought not to have children at all. They give *us* no pleasure.'

He was at that moment taking up the cup which Mrs. Tetterby had rudely pushed towards him, and Mrs. Tetterby was lifting her own cup to her lips, when they both stopped, as if they were transfixed.

'Here! Mother! Father!' cried Johnny, running into the room. 'Here's Mrs. William coming down the street!'

And if ever, since the world began, a young boy took a baby from a cradle with the care of an old nurse, and hushed and soothed it tenderly, and tottered away with it cheerfully, Johnny was that boy, and Moloch was that baby, as they went out together.

Mr. Tetterby put down his cup; Mrs. Tetterby put down

her cup. Mr. Tetterby rubbed his forehead; Mrs. Tetterby rubbed hers. Mr. Tetterby's face began to smooth and brighten; Mrs. Tetterby's began to smooth and brighten.

'Why, Lord forgive me,' said Mr. Tetterby to himself, 'what evil tempers have I been giving way to? What has been the matter here?'

'How could I ever treat him ill again, after all I said and felt last night?' sobbed Mrs. Tetterby, with her apron to her eyes.

'Am I a brute,' said Mr. Tetterby, 'or is there any good in me at all? Sophia! My little woman!'

''Dolphus dear!' returned his wife.

'I – I've been in a state of mind,' said Mr. Tetterby, 'that I can't bear to think of, Sophy.'

'Oh! It's nothing to what I've been in, Dolf,' cried his wife in a great burst of grief.

'My Sophia,' said Mr. Tetterby, 'don't take on! I never shall forgive myself. I must have nearly broke your heart, I know.'

'No, Dolf, no. It was me! Me!' cried Mrs. Tetterby.

'My little woman,' said her husband, 'don't. You make me reproach myself dreadful when you show such a noble spirit. Sophia, my dear, you don't know what I thought. I showed it bad enough, no doubt; but what I thought, my little woman —'

'Oh dear Dolf, don't! Don't!' cried his wife.

'Sophia,' said Mr. Tetterby, 'I must reveal it. I couldn't rest in my conscience unless I mentioned it. My little woman —'

'Mrs. William's very nearly here!' screamed Johnny at the door.

'My little woman, I wondered how,' gasped Mr. Tetterby, supporting himself by his chair, 'I wondered how I had ever admired you – I forgot the precious children you have brought about me, and thought you didn't look as slim as I could wish. I – I never gave a recollection,' said Mr. Tetterby with severe self-accusation, 'to the cares you've had as my wife, and along of me and mine, when you might have had hardly any with another man, who got on better and was luckier than me (anybody might have found such a man easily, I am sure); and I quarrelled with you for having aged a little in the rough years you've lightened for me. Can you believe it, my little woman? I hardly can myself.'

Mrs. Tetterby, in a whirlwind of laughing and crying, caught his face within her hands, and held it there.

'Oh, Dolf!' she cried. 'I am so happy that you thought so; I am so grateful that you thought so! For I thought that you were common-looking, Dolf; and so you are, my dear, and may you be the commonest of all sights in my eyes, till you close them with your own good hands! I thought that you were small; and so you are, and I'll make much of you because you are, and more of you because I love my husband. I thought that you began to stoop; and so you do, and you shall lean on me, and I'll do all I can to keep you up. I thought there was no air about you; but there is, and it's the air of home, and that's the purest and the best there is, and *God* bless home once more, and all belonging to it, Dolf!'

'Hurrah! Here's Mrs. William!' cried Johnny.

So she was, and all the children with her; and, as she came in, they kissed her, and kissed one another, and kissed the baby, and kissed their father and mother, and then ran back and flocked and danced about her, trooping on with her in triumph.

Mr. and Mrs. Tetterby were not a bit behind-hand in the warmth of their reception. They were as much attracted to her as the children were; they ran towards her, kissed her hands, pressed round her, could not receive her ardently or enthusiastically enough. She came among them like the spirit of all goodness, affection, gentle consideration, love, and domesticity.

'What! are *you* all so glad to see me, too, this bright Christmas morning?' said Milly, clapping her hands in a pleasant wonder. 'Oh dear, how delightful this is!'

More shouting from the children, more kissing, more trooping round her, more happiness, more love, more joy, more honour, on all sides, than she could bear.

'Oh dear!' said Milly, 'what delicious tears you make me shed! How can I ever have deserved this? What have I done to be so loved?'

'Who can help it?' cried Mr. Tetterby.

'Who can help it?' cried Mrs. Tetterby.

'Who can help it?' echoed the children in a joyful chorus. And they danced and trooped about her again, and clung to

her, and laid their rosy faces against her dress, and kissed and
fondled it, and could not fondle it, or her, enough.

'I never was so moved,' said Milly, drying her eyes, 'as I
have been this morning. I must tell you as soon as I can speak –
Mr. Redlaw came to me at sunrise, and with a tenderness in
his manner, more as if I had been his darling daughter than
myself, implored me to go with him to where William's
brother George is lying ill. We went together, and all the way
along he was so kind, and so subdued, and seemed to put such
trust and hope in me, that I could not help crying with
pleasure. When we got to the house, we met a woman at the
door (somebody had bruised and hurt her, I am afraid), who
caught me by the hand, and blessed me as I passed.'

'She was right,' said Mr. Tetterby. Mrs. Tetterby said she
was right. All the children cried out she was right.

'Ah! but there's more than that,' said Milly. 'When we got
upstairs into the room, the sick man, who had lain for hours in
a state from which no effort could rouse him, rose up in his
bed, and, bursting into tears, stretched out his arms to me, and
said that he had led a mis-spent life, but that he was truly
repentant now in his sorrow for the past, which was all as
plain to him as a great prospect from which a dense black
cloud had cleared away, and that he entreated me to ask his
poor old father for his pardon and his blessing, and to say a
prayer beside his bed. And, when I did so, Mr. Redlaw joined
in it so fervently, and then so thanked and thanked me, and
thanked Heaven, that my heart quite overflowed, and I could
have done nothing but sob and cry, if the sick man had not
begged me to sit down by him – which made me quiet, of
course. As I sat there, he held my hand in his until he sunk in a
doze; and even then, when I withdrew my hand to leave him
to come here (which Mr. Redlaw was very earnest indeed in
wishing me to do), his hand felt for mine, so that some one
else was obliged to take my place, and make believe to give
him my hand back. Oh dear oh dear!' said Milly, sobbing.
'How thankful and how happy I should feel, and do feel, for
all this!'

While she was speaking Redlaw had come in, and, after
pausing for a moment to observe the group of which she was
the centre, had silently ascended the stairs. Upon those stairs

he now appeared again; remaining there while the young student passed him, and came running down.

'Kind nurse, gentlest, best of creatures,' he said, falling on his knee to her, and catching at her hand, 'forgive my cruel ingratitude!'

'Oh dear, oh dear!' cried Milly innocently, 'here's another of them! Oh dear, here's somebody else who likes me! What shall I ever do?'

The guileless, simple way in which she said it, and in which she put her hands before her eyes and wept for very happiness, was as touching as it was delightful.

'I was not myself,' he said. 'I don't know what it was – it was some consequence of my disorder, perhaps – I was mad. But I am so no longer. Almost as I speak I am restored. I heard the children crying out your name, and the shade passed from me at the very sound of it. Oh, don't weep! Dear Milly, if you could read my heart, and only know with what affection and what grateful homage it is glowing, you would not let me see you weep. It is such deep reproach.'

'No, no,' said Milly, 'it's not that. It's not, indeed. It's joy. It's wonder that you should think it necessary to ask me to forgive so little, and yet it's pleasure that you do.'

'And will you come again? and will you finish the little curtain?'

'No,' said Milly, drying her eyes, and shaking her head. 'You won't care for *my* needlework now.'

'Is it forgiving me to say that?'

She beckoned him aside, and whispered in his ear.

'There is news from your home, Mr. Edmund.'

'News? How?'

'Either your not writing when you were very ill, or the change in your handwriting when you began to be better, created some suspicion of the truth. However, that is — But you're sure you'll not be the worse for any news, if it's not bad news?'

'Sure.'

'Then there's some one come!' said Milly.

'My mother?' asked the student, glancing round involuntarily towards Redlaw, who had come down from the stairs.

'Hush! No,' said Milly.

'It can be no one else.'

'Indeed!' said Milly. 'Are you sure?'

'It is not —' Before he could say more, she put her hand upon his mouth.

'Yes, it is!' said Milly. 'The young lady (she is very like the miniature, Mr. Edmund, but she is prettier) was too unhappy to rest without satisfying her doubts, and came up last night, with a little servant-maid. As you always dated your letters from the College, she came there; and, before I saw Mr. Redlaw this morning, I saw her. *She* likes me too!' said Milly. 'Oh dear, that's another!'

'This morning! Where is she now?'

'Why, she is now,' said Milly advancing her lips to his ear, 'in my little parlour in the Lodge, and waiting to see you.'

He pressed her hand, and was darting off, but she detained him.

'Mr. Redlaw is much altered, and has told me this morning that his memory is impaired. Be very considerate to him, Mr. Edmund; he needs that from us all.'

The young man assured her, by a look, that her caution was not ill bestowed; and, as he passed the Chemist on his way out, bent respectfully and with an obvious interest before him.

Redlaw returned the salutation courteously, and even humbly, and looked after him as he passed on. He dropped his head upon his hand too, as if trying to re-awaken something he had lost. But it was gone.

The abiding change that had come upon him since the influence of the music, and the Phantom's reappearance, was, that now he truly felt how much he had lost, and could compassionate his own condition, and contrast it, clearly, with the natural state of those who were around him. In this, an interest in those who were around him was revived, and a meek, submissive sense of his calamity was bred, resembling that which sometimes obtains in age, when its mental powers are weakened without insensibility or sullenness being added to the list of its infirmities.

He was conscious that, as he redeemed, through Milly, more and more of the evil he had done, and as he was more and more with her, this change ripened itself within him. Therefore, and because of the attachment she inspired him with (but without other hope), he felt that he was quite dependent on her, and that she was his staff in his affliction.

So, when she asked him whether they should go home now to where the old man and her husband were, and he readily replied, 'Yes' – being anxious in that regard – he put his arm through hers, and walked beside her; not as if he were the wise and learned man to whom the wonders of nature were an open book, and hers were the uninstructed mind, but as if their two positions were reversed, and he knew nothing, and she all.

He saw the children throng about her, and caress her, as he and she went away together thus out of the house; he heard the ringing of their laughter, and their merry voices; he saw their bright faces clustering round him like flowers, he witnessed the renewed contentment and affection of their parents; he breathed the simple air of their poor home, restored to its tranquillity; he thought of the unwholesome blight he had shed upon it, and might, but for her, have been diffusing then; and perhaps it is no wonder that he walked submissively beside her, and drew her gentle bosom nearer to his own.

When they arrived at the Lodge, the old man was sitting in his chair in the chimney-corner, with his eyes fixed on the ground, and his son was leaning against the opposite side of the fire-place, looking at him. As she came in at the door, both started and turned round towards her, and a radiant change came upon their faces.

'Oh dear, dear, dear, they are pleased to see me, like the rest!' cried Milly, clapping her hands in an ecstasy, and stopping short. 'Here are two more!'

Pleased to see her! Pleasure was no word for it. She ran into her husband's arms, thrown wide open to receive her, and he would have been glad to have her there, with her head lying on his shoulder, through the short winter's day. But the old man couldn't spare her. He had arms for her too, and he locked her in them.

'Why, where has my quiet Mouse been all this time?' said the old man. 'She has been a long while away. I find that it's impossible for me to get on without Mouse. I – where's my son William? – I fancy I have been dreaming, William.'

'That's what I say myself, father,' returned his son. '*I* have been in an ugly sort of dream, I think. How are you, father? Are you pretty well?'

'Strong and brave, my boy,' returned the old man.

It was quite a sight to see Mr. William shaking hands with his father, and patting him on the back, and rubbing him gently down with his hand, as if he could not possibly do enough to show an interest in him.

'What a wonderful man you are, father! How are you father? Are you really pretty hearty, though?' said William, shaking hands with him again, and patting him again, and rubbing him gently down again.

'I never was fresher or stouter in my life, my boy.'

'What a wonderful man you are, father! But that's exactly where it is,' said Mr. William with enthusiasm. 'When I think of all that my father's gone through, and all the chances and changes, and sorrows and troubles, that have happened to him in the course of his long life, and under which his head has grown grey, and years upon years have gathered on it, I feel as if we couldn't do enough to honour the old gentleman, and make his old age easy. How are you, father? Are you really pretty well, though?'

Mr. William might never have left off repeating his inquiry and shaking hands with him again, and patting him again, and rubbing him down again, if the old man had not espied the Chemist, whom until now he had not seen.

'I ask your pardon, Mr. Redlaw,' said Philip, 'but didn't know you were here, sir, or should have made less free. It reminds me, Mr. Redlaw, seeing you here on a Christmas morning, of the time when you was a student yourself, and worked so hard that you was backwards and forwards in our library even at Christmas-time. Ha, ha! I'm old enough to remember that; and I remember it right well, I do, though I am eighty-seven. It was after you left here that my poor wife died. You remember my poor wife, Mr. Redlaw?'

The Chemist answered, 'Yes.'

'Yes,' said the old man. 'She was a dear creetur. — I recollect you come here one Christmas morning with a young lady – I ask your pardon Mr. Redlaw, but I think it was a sister you was very much attached to?'

The Chemist looked at him, and shook his head. 'I had a

sister,' he said vacantly. He knew no more.

'One Christmas morning,' pursued the old man, 'that you come here with her – and it began to snow, and my wife invited the young lady to walk in, and sit by the fire that is always a burning on Christmas Day in what used to be, before our ten poor gentlemen commuted, our great Dinner Hall. I was there; and I recollect, as I was stirring up the blaze for the young lady to warm her pretty feet by, she read the scroll out loud, that is underneath that picter. "Lord, keep my memory green!" She and my poor wife fell a talking about it; and it's a strange thing to think of, now, that they both said (both being so unlike to die) that it was a good prayer, and that it was one they would put up very earnestly, if they were called away young, with reference to those who were dearest to them. "My brother," says the young lady – "My husband," says my poor wife – "Lord, keep his memory of me green, and do not let me be forgotten!"'

Tears more painful and more bitter than he had ever shed in all his life coursed down Redlaw's face. Philip, fully occupied in recalling his story, had not observed him until now, nor Milly's anxiety that he should not proceed.

'Philip!' said Redlaw, laying his hand upon his arm, 'I am a stricken man, on whom the hand of Providence has fallen heavily, although deservedly. You speak to me, my friend, of what I cannot follow; my memory is gone.'

'Merciful power!' cried the old man.

'I have lost my memory of sorrow, wrong, and trouble,' said the Chemist; 'and with that I have lost all man would remember!'

To see old Philip's pity for him, to see him wheel his own great chair for him to rest in, and look down upon him with a solemn sense of his bereavement, was to know, in some degree, how precious to old age such recollections are.

The boy came running in, and ran to Milly.

'Here's the man,' he said, 'in the other room. I don't want *him*.'

'What man does he mean?' asked Mr. William.

'Hush!' said Milly.

Obedient to a sign from her, he and his old father softly

withdrew. As they went out unnoticed, Redlaw beckoned to the boy to come to him.

'I like the woman best,' he answered holding to her skirts.

'You are right,' said Redlaw with a faint smile. 'But you needn't fear to come to me. I am gentler than I was. Of all the world, to you, poor child!'

The boy still held back at first; but yielding little by little to her urging, he consented to approach, and even to sit down at his feet. As Redlaw laid his hand upon the shoulder of the child, looking on him with compassion and a fellow-feeling, he put out his other hand to Milly. She stooped down on that side of him, so that she could look into his face; and, after silence, said: 'Mr. Redlaw, may I speak to you?'

'Yes,' he answered, fixing his eyes upon her. 'Your voice and music are the same to me.'

'May I ask you something?'

'What you will.'

'Do you remember what I said when I knocked at your door last night? About one who was your friend once, and who stood on the verge of destruction?'

'Yes. I remember,' he said with some hesitation.

'Do you understand it?'

He smoothed the boy's hair – looking at her fixedly the while, and shook his head.

'This person,' said Milly in her clear, soft voice, which her mild eyes, looking at him, made clearer and softer, 'I found soon afterwards. I went back to the house, and, with Heaven's help, traced him. I was not too soon. A very little, and I should have been too late.'

He took his hand from the boy, and, laying it on the back of that hand of hers, whose timid and yet earnest touch addressed him no less appealingly than her voice and eyes, looked more intently on her.

'He *is* the father of Mr. Edmund, the young gentleman we saw just now. His real name is Langford. – You recollect the name?'

'I recollect the name.'

'And the man?'

'No, not the man. Did he ever wrong me?'

'Yes!'

'Ah! Then it's hopeless – hopeless.'

He shook his head, and softly beat upon the hand he held, as though mutely asking her commiseration.

'I did not go to Mr. Edmund last night,' said Milly. 'You will listen to me just the same as if you did remember all?'

'To every syllable you say.'

'Both because I did not know, then, that this really was his father, and because I was fearful of the effect of such intelligence upon him, after his illness, if it should be. Since I have known who this person is, I have not gone either; but that is for another reason. He has long been separated from his wife and son – has been a stranger to his home almost from his son's infancy, I learn from him – and has abandoned and deserted what he should have held most dear. In all that time he has been falling from the state of a gentleman, more and more, until —' She rose up hastily, and, going out for a moment, returned, accompanied by the wreck that Redlaw had beheld last night.

'Do you know me?' asked the Chemist.

'I should be glad,' returned the other, 'and that is an unwonted word for me to use, if I could answer no.'

The Chemist looked at the man standing, in self-abasement and degradation before him, and would have looked longer, in an ineffectual struggle for enlightenment, but that Milly resumed her late position by his side, and attracted his attentive gaze to her own face.

'See how low he is sunk, how lost he is!' she whispered, stretching out her arm towards him, without looking from the Chemist's face. 'If you could remember all that is connected with him, do you not think it would move your pity to reflect that one you ever loved (do not let us mind how long ago, or in what belief that he has forfeited), should come to this?'

'I hope it would,' he answered. 'I believe it would.'

His eyes wandered to the figure standing near the door, but came back speedily to her, on whom he gazed intently, as if he strove to learn some lesson from every tone of her voice, and every beam of her eyes.

'I have no learning, and you have much,' said Milly; 'I am not used to think, and you are always thinking. May I tell you why it seems to me a good thing for us to remember wrong that has been done us?'

'Yes.'

'That we may forgive it.'

'Pardon me, great Heaven!' said Redlaw, lifting up his eyes, 'for having thrown away thine own high attribute!'

'And if,' said Milly, 'if your memory should one day be restored, as we will hope and pray it may be, would it not be a blessing to you to recall at once a wrong and its forgiveness?'

He looked at the figure by the door, and fastened his attentive eyes on her again. A ray of clearer light appeared to him to shine into his mind from her bright face.

'He cannot go to his abandoned home. He does not seek to go there. He knows that he could only carry shame and trouble to those he has so cruelly neglected; and that the best reparation he can make them now is to avoid them. A very little money, carefully bestowed, would remove him to some distant place, where he might live and do no wrong, and make such atonement as is left within his power for the wrong he has done. To the unfortunate lady who is his wife, and to his son, this would be the best and kindest boon that their best friend could give them – one, too, that they need never know of; and to him, shattered in reputation, mind, and body, it might be salvation.'

He took her head between his hands, and kissed it, and said: 'It shall be done. I trust to you to do it for me, now and secretly; and to tell him that I would forgive him, if I were so happy as to know for what.'

As she rose, and turned her beaming face towards the fallen man, implying that her mediation had been successful, he advanced a step, and, without raising his eyes, addressed himself to Redlaw.

'You are so generous,' he said, 'you ever were – that you will try to banish your rising sense of retribution in the spectacle that is before you. I do not try to banish it from myself, Redlaw. If you can, believe me.'

The Chemist entreated Milly, by a gesture, to come nearer to him; and, as he listened, looked in her face, as if to find in it the clue to what he heard.

'I am too decayed a wretch to make professions; I recollect

my own career too well to array any such before you. But
from the day on which I made my first step downward, in
dealing falsely by you, I have gone down with a certain,
steady, doomed progression. That I say.'

Redlaw, keeping her close at his side, turned his face
towards the speaker, and there was sorrow in it. Something
like mournful recognition too.

'I might have been another man, my life might have been
another life, if I had avoided that first fatal step. I don't know
that it would have been. I claim nothing for the possibility.
Your sister is at rest, and better than she could have been with
me, if I had continued even what you thought me: even what I
once supposed myself to be.'

Redlaw made a hasty motion with his hand, as if he would
have put that subject on one side.

'I speak,' the other went on, 'like a man taken from the
grave. I should have made my own grave last night, had it not
been for this blessed hand.'

'Oh dear, he likes me too!' sobbed Milly under her breath.
'That's another!'

'I could not have put myself in your way last night, even for
bread. But, today, my recollection of what has been between
us is so strongly stirred, and is presented to me, I don't know
how, so vividly, that I have dared to come at her suggestion,
and to take your bounty, and to thank you for it, and beg you,
Redlaw, in your dying hour, to be as merciful to me in your
thoughts as you are in your deeds.'

He turned towards the door, and stopped a moment on his
way forth.

'I hope my son may interest you, for his mother's sake. I
hope he may deserve to do so. Unless my life should be
preserved a long time, and I should know that I have not
misused your aid, I shall never look upon him more.'

Going out, he raised his eyes to Redlaw for the first time.
Redlaw, whose steadfast gaze was fixed upon him, dreamily
held out his hand. He returned and touched it – little more –
with both his own – and, bending down his head, went slowly
out.

In the few moments that elapsed while Milly silently took
him to the gate, the Chemist dropped into his chair, and

covered his face with his hands. Seeing him thus when she came back, accompanied by her husband and his father (who were both greatly concerned for him), she avoided disturbing him, or permitting him to be disturbed; and kneeled down near the chair to put some warm clothing on the boy.

'That's exactly where it is. That's what I always say, father!' exclaimed her admiring husband. 'There's a motherly feeling in Mrs. William's breast that must and will have went!'

'Ay, ay,' said the old man; 'you're right. My son William's right!'

'It happens all for the best, Milly dear, no doubt,' said Mr. William tenderly, 'that we have no children of our own; and yet I sometimes wish you had one to love and cherish. Our little dead child that you built such hopes upon, and that never breathed the breath of life – it has made you quiet-like, Milly.'

'I am very happy in the recollection of it, William dear,' she answered. 'I think of it every day.'

'I was afraid you thought of it a good deal.'

'Don't say afraid; it is a comfort to me; it speaks to me in so many ways. The innocent thing that never lived on earth is like an angel to me, William.'

'You are like an angel to father and me,' said Mr. William softly. 'I know that.'

'When I think of all those hopes I built upon it, and the many times I sat and pictured to myself the little smiling face upon my bosom, that never lay there, and the sweet eyes turned up to mine that never opened to the light,' said Milly, 'I can feel a greater tenderness, I think, for all the disappointed hopes in which there is no harm. When I see a beautiful child in its fond mother's arms, I love it all the better, thinking that my child might have been like that, and might have made my heart as proud and happy.'

Redlaw raised his head, and looked towards her.

'All through life, it seems by me,' she continued, 'to tell me something. For poor neglected children my little child pleads as if it were alive, and had a voice I knew, with which to speak to me. When I hear of youth in suffering or shame, I think that my child might have come to that, perhaps, and that God took it from me in his mercy. Even in age and grey hair, such as father's, it is present: saying that it too might have lived to be old, long and long after you and I were gone, and to have needed the respect and love of younger people.'

Her quiet voice was quieter than ever as she took her husband's arm, and laid her head against it.

'Children love me so, that sometimes I half fancy – it's a silly fancy, William – they have some way I don't know of, of feeling for my little child, and me, and understanding why their love is precious to me. If I have been quiet since, I have been more happy, William, in a hundred ways. Not least happy, dear, in this – that even when my little child was born and dead but a few days, and I was weak and sorrowful, and could not help grieving a little, the thought arose that, if I tried to lead a good life, I should meet in Heaven a bright creature who would call me Mother!'

Redlaw fell upon his knees with a loud cry.

'O Thou,' he said, 'who, through the teaching of pure love, hast graciously restored me to the memory which was the memory of Christ upon the cross, and of all the good who perished in His cause, receive my thanks, and bless her!'

Then he folded her to his heart; and Milly, sobbing more than ever, cried, as she laughed. 'He is come back to himself! He likes me very much indeed, too! Oh dear, dear, dear me, here's another!'

Then, the student entered, leading by the hand a lovely girl, who was afraid to come. And Redlaw, so changed towards him, seeing in him, and in his youthful choice, the softened shadow of that chastening passage in his own life, to which, as to a shady tree, the dove so long imprisoned in his solitary ark might fly for rest and company, fell upon his neck, entreating them to be his children.

Then, as Christmas is a time in which, of all times in the year, the memory of every remediable sorrow, wrong, and trouble in the world around us, should be active with us, not less than our own experiences, for all good, he laid his hand upon the boy, and, silently calling Him to witness who laid His hand on children in old time, rebuking, in the majesty of His prophetic knowledge, those who kept them from him, vowed to protect him, teach him, and reclaim him.

Then, he gave his right hand cheerily to Philip, and said that they would that day hold a Christmas dinner in what used to be, before the ten poor gentlemen commuted, their great Dinner Hall; and that they would bid to it as many of that Swidger family, who, his son had told him, were so numerous that they might join hands and make a ring round England, as could be brought together on so short a notice.

And it was that day done. There were so many Swidgers there, grown up and children, that an attempt to state them in round numbers might engender doubts, in the distrustful, of the veracity of this history. Therefore the attempts shall not be made. But there they were, by dozens and scores – and there was good news and good hope there, ready for them, of George, who had been visited again by his father and brother, and by Milly, and again left in a quiet sleep. There, present at the dinner too, were the Tetterbys, including young Adolphus, who arrived in his prismatic comforter, in good time for the beef. Johnny and the baby were too late, of course, and came in all on one side, the one exhausted, the other in a supposed state of double-tooth; but that was customary, and not alarming.

It was sad to see the child who had no name or lineage watching the other children as they played, not knowing how to talk with them, or sport with them, and more strange to the ways of childhood than a rough dog. It was sad, though in a different way, to see what an instinctive knowledge the youngest child there had of his being different from the rest, and how they made timid approaches to him with soft words and with touches, and with little presents, that he might not be unhappy. But he kept by Milly, and began to love her – that was another, as she said! – and, as they all liked her dearly, they were glad of that, and when they saw him peeping at them from behind her chair, they were pleased that he was so close to it.

All this the Chemist, sitting with the student and his bride that was to be, and Philip, and the rest, saw.

Some people have said since that he only thought what has been herein set down; others, that he read it in the fire, one winter night about the twilight-time; others, that the Ghost was but the representation of his gloomy thoughts, and Milly the embodiment of his better wisdom. *I* say nothing.

— Except this. That as they were assembled in the old Hall,

by no other light than that of a great fire (having dined early), the shadows once more stole out of their hiding-places, and danced about the room, showing the children marvellous shapes and faces on the walls, and gradually changing what was real and familiar there to what was wild and magical. But that there was one thing in the Hall to which the eyes of Redlaw, and of Milly and her husband, and of the old man, and of the student, and his bride that was to be, were often turned, which the shadows did not obscure or change. Deepened in its gravity by the fire-light, and gazing from the darkness of the panelled wall like life, the sedate face in the portrait, with the beard and ruff, looked down at them from under its verdant wreath of holly, as they looked up at it, and, clear and plain below, as if a voice had uttered them, were the words:

'Lord, keep my Memory Green!'

THE HAUNTED HOUSE

THE MORTALS IN THE HOUSE

Under none of the accredited ghostly circumstances, and environed by none of the conventional ghostly surroundings, did I first make acquaintance with the house which is the subject of this Christmas piece. I saw it in the daylight, with the sun upon it. There was no wind, no rain, no lightning, no thunder, no awful or unwonted circumstance, of any kind, to heighten its effect. More than that: I had come to it direct from a railway station: it was not more than a mile distant from the railway station; and, as I stood outside the house, looking back upon the way I had come, I could see the goods train running smoothly along the embankment in the valley. I will not say that everything was utterly commonplace, because I doubt if anything can be that, except to utterly commonplace people – and there my vanity steps in; but, I will take it on myself to say that anybody might see the house as I saw it, any fine autumn morning.

The manner of my lighting on it was this.

I was travelling towards London out of the North, intending to stop by the way, to look at the house. My health required a temporary residence in the country; and a friend of mine who knew that, and who had happened to drive past the house, had written to me to suggest it as a likely place. I had got into the train at midnight, and had fallen asleep, and had woke up and had sat looking out of window at the brillant Northern Lights in the sky, and had fallen asleep again, and had woke up again to find the night gone, with the usual discontented conviction on me that I hadn't been to sleep at all; – upon which question, in the first imbecility of that condition, I am ashamed to believe that I would have done wager by battle with the man who sat opposite me. That opposite man had had, through the night – as that opposite man always has – several legs too many, and all of them too long. In addition to this unreasonable conduct (which was only to be expected of him), he had had a pencil and a pocket-book, and had been perpetually listening and taking notes. It had appeared to me that these aggravating notes related to the jolts and bumps of the carriage, and I should have resigned myself to his taking them, under a general supposition that he was in the civil-engineering way of life, if he had not sat staring straight over my head whenever he listened. He was a goggly-eyed gentleman of a perplexed aspect, and his demeanour became unbearable.

It was a cold, dead morning (the sun not being up yet), and when I had out-watched the paling light of the fires of the iron country, and the curtain of heavy smoke that hung at once between me and the stars and between me and the day, I turned to my fellow-traveller and said:

'I *beg* your pardon, Sir, but do you observe anything particular in me?' For, really, he appeared to be taking down, either my travelling-cap or my hair, with a minuteness that was a liberty.

The goggle-eyed gentleman withdrew his eyes from behind me, as if the back of the carriage were a hundred miles off, and said, with a lofty look of compassion for my insignificance:

'In you, Sir? – B.'

'B, Sir?' said I, growing warm.

'I have nothing to do with you, Sir,' returned the gentleman; 'pray let me listen – O.'

He enunciated this vowel after a pause, and noted it down.

At first I was alarmed, for an Express lunatic and no communication with the guard, is a serious position. The thought came to my relief that the gentleman might be what is popularly called a Rapper: one of a sect for (some of) whom I have the highest respect, but whom I don't believe in. I was going to ask him the question, when he took the bread out of my mouth.

'You will excuse me,' said the gentleman contemptuously, 'if I am too much in advance of common humanity to trouble myself at all about it. I have passed the night – as indeed I pass the whole of my time now – in spiritual intercourse.'

'O!' said I, something snappishly.

'The conferences of the night began,' continued the gentleman, turning several leaves of his note-book, 'with this message: "Evil communications corrupt good manners."'

'Sound,' said I; 'but, absolutely new?'

'New from spirits,' returned the gentleman.

I could only repeat my rather snappish 'O!' and ask if I might be favoured with the last communication.

"A bird in the hand," said the gentleman, reading his last entry with great solemnity, "is worth two in the Bosh."

'Truly I am of the same opinion,' said I; 'but shouldn't it be Bush?'

'It came to me, Bosh,' returned the gentleman.

The gentleman then informed me that the spirit of Socrates had delivered this special revelation in the course of the night, 'My friend, I hope you are pretty well. There are two in this railway carriage. How do you do? There are seventeen thousand four hundred and seventy-nine spirits here, but you cannot see them. Pythagoras is here. He is not at liberty to mention it, but hopes you like travelling.' Galileo likewise had dropped in, with this scientific intelligence. 'I am glad to see you, *amico. Come sta?* Water will freeze when it is cold enough. *Addio!*' In the course of the night, also, the following phenomena had occurred. Bishop Butler had insisted on spelling his name, 'Bubler,' for which offence against orthography and good manners he had been dismissed as out of temper. John Milton (suspected of wilful mystification) had repudiated the authorship of Paradise Lost, and had introduced, as joint authors of that poem, two Unknown gentlemen, respectively named Grungers and Scadgingtone. And Prince Arthur, nephew of King John of England, had described himself as tolerably comfortable in the seventh circle, where he was learning to paint on velvet, under the direction of Mrs. Trimmer and Mary Queen of Scots.

If this should meet the eye of the gentleman who favoured me with these disclosures, I trust he will excuse my confessing that the sight of the rising sun, and the contemplation of the magnificent Order of the vast Universe, made me impatient of them. In a word, I was so impatient of them, that I was mightily glad to get out at the next station, and to exchange these clouds and vapours for the free air of Heaven.

By that time it was a beautiful morning. As I walked away among such leaves as had already fallen from the golden, brown, and russet trees; and as I looked around me on the wonders of Creation, and thought of the steady, unchanging, and harmonious laws by which they are sustained; the gentleman's spiritual intercourse seemed to me as poor a piece of journey-work as ever this world saw. In which heathen state of mind, I came within view of the house, and stopped to examine it attentively.

It was a solitary house, standing in a sadly neglected garden: a pretty even square of some two acres. It was a house of about the time of George the Second; as stiff, as cold, as formal, and in as bad taste, as could possibly be desired by the most loyal admirer of the whole quartet of Georges. It was uninhabited, but had, within a year or two, been cheaply repaired to render it habitable; I say cheaply, because the work had been done in a surface manner, and was already decaying as to the paint and plaster, though the colours were fresh. A lop-sided board drooped over the garden wall, announcing that it was 'to let on very reasonable terms, well furnished.' It was much too closely and heavily shadowed by trees, and, in particular, there were six tall poplars before the front windows, which were excessively melancholy, and the site of which had been extremely ill chosen.

It was easy to see that it was an avoided house – a house that was shunned by the village, to which my eye was guided by a church spire some half a mile off – a house that nobody would take. And the natural inference was, that it had the reputation of being a haunted house.

No period within the four-and twenty hours of day and night is so solemn to me, as the early morning. In the summer time, I often rise very early, and repair to my room to do a day's work before breakfast, and I am always on those occasions deeply impressed by the stillness and solitude around me. Besides that there is something awful in the being surrounded by familiar faces asleep – in the knowledge that those who are dearest to us and to whom we are dearest, are profoundly unconscious of us, in an impassive state, anticipative of that mysterious condition to which we are all tending – the stopped life, the broken threads of yesterday, the deserted seat, the closed book, the unfinished but abandoned occupation, all are images of Death. The tranquillity of the hour is the tranquillity of Death. The colour and the chill have the same association. Even a certain air that familiar household objects take upon them when they first emerge from the shadows of the night into the morning, of being newer, and as they used to be long ago, has its counterpart in the subsidence of the worn face of maturity or age, in death, into the old youthful look. Moreover, I once saw the apparition of my father, at this hour. He was alive and well, and nothing ever came of it, but I saw him in the daylight, sitting with his back towards me, on a seat that stood beside my bed. His head was resting on his hand, and whether he was slumbering or grieving, I could not discern. Amazed to see him there, I sat up, moved my position, leaned out of bed, and watched him. As he did not move then, I became alarmed and laid my hand upon his shoulder, as I thought – and there was no such thing.

For all these reasons, and for others less easily and briefly statable, I find the early morning to be my most ghostly time. Any house would be more or less haunted, to me, in the early morning; and a haunted house could scarcely address me to greater advantage than then.

I walked on into the village, with the desertion of this house upon my mind, and I found the landlord of the little inn, sanding his doorstep. I bespoke breakfast, and broached the subject of the house.

'Is it haunted?' I asked.

The landlord looked at me, shook his head, and answered, 'I say nothing.'

'Then it is haunted?'

'Well!' cried the landlord, in a outburst of frankness that had the appearances of desperation – 'I wouldn't sleep in it.'

'Why not?'

'If I wanted to have all the bells in a house ring, with nobody to ring 'em; and all the doors in a house bang, with nobody to bang 'em; and all sorts of feet treading about, with no feet there; why, then,' said the landlord. 'I'd sleep in that house.'

'Is anything seen there?'

The landlord looked at me again, and then, with his former appearance of desperation, called down his stable-yard for 'Ikey!'

The call produced a high-shouldered young fellow, with a round red face, a short crop of sandy hair, a very broad humerous mouth, a turned-up nose, and a great sleeved waistcoat of purple bars, with mother-of-pearl buttons, that seemed to be growing upon him, and to be in a fair way – if it were not pruned – of covering his head and overrunning his boots.

'This gentleman wants to know,' said the landlord, 'if anything's seen at the Poplars.'

''Ooded woman with a howl,' said Ikey, in a state of great freshness.

'Do you mean a cry?'

'I mean a bird, Sir.'

'A hooded woman with an owl. Dear me! Did you ever see her?'

'I seen the howl.'

'Never the woman?'

'Not so plain as the howl, but they always keeps together.'

'Has anybody ever seen the woman as plainly as the owl?'

'Lord bless you, Sir! Lots.'

'Who?'

'Lord bless you, Sir! Lots.'

'The general-dealer opposite, for instance, who is opening his shop?'

'Perkins? Bless you, Perkins wouldn't go a-nigh the place. No!' observed the young man, with considerable feeling; 'he an't over wise, an't Perkins, but he an't such a fool as *that*.'

(Here, the landlord murmured his confidence in Perkins's knowing better.)

'Who is – or who was – the hooded woman with the owl? Do you know?'

'Well!' said Ikey, holding up his cap with one hand while he scratched his head with the other, 'they say, in general, that she was murdered, and the howl he 'ooted the while.'

This very concise summary of the facts was all I could learn, except that a young man, as hearty and likely a young man as ever I see, had been took with fits and held down in 'em, after seeing the hooded woman. Also, that a personage, dimly described as 'a hold chap, a sort of one-eyed tramp, answering to the name of Joby, unless you challenged him as Greenwood, and then he said, 'Why not? and even if so, mind your own business,'' had encountered the hooded woman, a matter of five or six times. But, I was not materially assisted by these witnesses: inasmuch as the first was in California, and the last was, as Ikey said (and he was confirmed by the landlord), Anywheres.

Now, although I regard with a hushed and solemn fear, the mysteries, between which and this state of existence is interposed the barrier of the great trial and change that fall on all the things that live; and although I have not the audacity to pretend that I know anything of them; I can no more reconcile the more banging of doors, ringing of bells, creaking of boards, and such-like insignificances, with the majestic beauty and pervading analogy of all the Divine rules that I am permitted to understand, than I had been able, a little while before, to yoke the spiritual intercourse of my fellow-traveller to the chariot of the rising sun. Moreover, I had lived in two haunted houses – both abroad. In one of these, an old Italian palace, which bore the reputation of being twice abandoned on that account, I lived eight months, most tranquilly and pleasantly: notwithstanding that the house had a score of mysterious bedrooms, which were never used, and possessed, in one large room in which I sat reading, times out of number at all hours, and next to which I slept, a haunted chamber of the first pretensions. I gently hinted these considerations to the landlord. And as to this particular house having a bad name, I reasoned with him, Why, how many things had bad names undeservedly, and how easy it was to give bad names, and did he not think that if he and I were persistently to whisper in the village that any weird-looking old drunken tinker of the neighbourhood had sold himself to the Devil, he would come in time to be suspected, of that commercial venture! All this wise talk was perfectly ineffective with the landlord, I am bound to confess, and was as dead a failure as ever I made in my life.

To cut this part of the story short, I was piqued about the haunted house, and was already half resolved to take it. So, after breakfast, I got the keys from Perkins's brother-in-law (a whip and harness maker, who keeps the Post Office, and is under submission to a most rigorous wife of the Doubly

Seceding Little Emmanuel persuasion), and went up to the house, attended by my landlord and by Ikey.

Within, I found it, as I had expected, transcendently dismal. The slowly changing shadows waved on it from the heavy trees, were doleful in the last degree; the house was ill-placed, ill-built, ill-planned, and ill-fitted. It was damp, it was not free from dry rot, there was a flavour of rats in it, and it was the gloomy victim of that indescribable decay which settles on all the work of man's hands whenever it is not turned to man's account. The kitchens and offices were too large, and too remote from each other. Above stairs and below, waste tracts of passage intervened between patches of fertility represented by rooms; and there was a mouldy old well with a green growth upon it, hiding like a murderous trap, near the bottom of the back stairs, under the double row of bells. One of these bells was labelled, on a black ground in faded white letters, MASTER B. This, they told me, was the bell that rang the most.

'Who was Master B.?' I asked. 'Is it known what he did while the owl hooted?'

'Rang the bell,' said Ikey.

I was rather struck by the prompt dexterity with which this young man pitched his fur cap at the bell, and rang it himself. It was a loud, unpleasant bell, and made a very disagreeable sound. The other bells were inscribed according to the names of the rooms to which their wires were conducted: as 'Picture Room,' 'Double Room,' 'Clock Room,' and the like. Following Master B.'s bell to its source, I found that young gentleman to have had but indifferent third-class accommodation in a triangular cabin under the cock-loft, with a corner fireplace which Master B. must have been exceedingly small if he were ever able to warm himself at, and a corner chimneypiece like a pyramidal staircase to the ceiling for Tom Thumb. The papering of one side of the room had dropped down bodily, with fragments of plaster adhering to it, and almost blocked up the door. It appeared that Master B., in his spiritual condition, always made a point of pulling the paper down. Neither the landlord nor Ikey could suggest why he made such a fool of himself.

Except that the house had an immensely large rambling loft

at top, I made no other discoveries. It was moderately well furnished, but sparely. Some of the furniture – say, a third – was as old as the house; the rest was of various periods within the last half-century. I was referred to a corn-chandler in the market-place of the country town to treat for the house. I went that day, and I took it for six months.

It was just the middle of October when I moved in with my maiden sister (I venture to call her eight-and-thirty, she is so very handsome, sensible, and engaging). We took with us, a deaf stable-man, my bloodhound Turk, two women servants, and a young person called an Odd Girl. I have reason to record of the attendant last enumerated, who was one of the Saint Lawrence's Union Female Orphans, that she was a fatal mistake and a disastrous engagement.

The year was dying early, the leaves were falling fast, it was a raw cold day when we took possession, and the gloom of the house was most depressing. The cook (an amiable woman, but of a weak turn of intellect) burst into tears on beholding the kitchen, and requested that her silver watch might be delivered over to her sister (2 Tuppintock's Gardens, Liggs's Walk, Clapham Rise), in the event of anything happening to her from the damp. Streaker, the housemaid, feigned cheerfulness, but was the greater martyr. The Odd Girl, who had never been in the country, alone was pleased and made arrangements for sowing an acorn in the garden outside the scullery window, and rearing an oak.

We went, before dark, through all the natural – as opposed to supernatural – miseries incidental to our state. Dispiriting reports ascended (like the smoke) from the basement in no rolling-pin, there was no salamander (which failed to surprise me, for I don't know what it is), there was nothing in the house, what there was, was broken, the last people must have lived like pigs, what could the meaning of the landlord be? Through these distresses, the Odd Girl was cheerful and exemplary. But within four hours after dark we had got into a supernatural groove, and the Odd Girl had seen 'Eyes,' and was in hysterics.

My sister and I had agreed to keep the haunting strictly to ourselves, and my impression was, and still is, that I had not left Ikey, when he helped to unload the cart, alone with the woman, or any one of them, for one minute. Nevertheless, as I say, the Odd Girl had 'seen Eyes' (no other explanation could ever be drawn from her), before nine, and by ten o'clock had had as much vinegar applied to her as would pickle a handsome salmon.

I leave a discerning public to judge of my feelings, when, under these untoward circumstances, at about half-past ten o'clock Master B.'s bell began to ring in a most infuriated manner, and Turk howled until the house resounded with his lamentations!

I hope I may never again be in a state of mind so unchristian as the mental frame in which I lived for some weeks, respecting the memory of Master B. Whether his bell was rung by rats, or mice, or bats, or wind, or what other accidental vibration or sometimes by one cause, sometimes another, and sometimes by collusion, I don't know; but, certain it is, that it did ring two nights out of three, until I conceived the happy idea of twisting Master B.'s neck – in other words, breaking his bell short off – and silencing that young gentleman, as to my experience and belief, for ever.

But, by that time, the Odd Girl had developed such improving powers of catalepsy, that she had become a shining example of that very inconvenient disorder. She would stiffen, like a Guy Fawkes endowed with unreason, on the most irrelevant occasions. I would address the servants in a lucid manner, pointing out to them that I had painted Master B.'s room and balked the paper, and taken Master B.'s bell away and balked the ringing, and if they could suppose that that confounded boy had lived and died, to clothe himself with no better behaviour than would most unquestionably have brought him and the sharpest particles of a birch-broom into close acquaintance in the present imperfect state of existence, could they also suppose a mere poor human being, such as I was, capable by those contemptible means of counteracting and limiting the powers of the disembodied spirits of the dead, or of any spirits? – I say I would become emphatic and cogent, not to say rather complacent, in such an address, when it would all go for nothing by reason of the Odd Girl's suddenly stiffening from the toes upward, and glaring amoung us like a parochial petrifaction.

Streaker, the housemaid, too, had an attribute of a most discomfiting nature. I am unable to say whether she was of an unusually lymphatic temperament, or what else was the matter with her, but this young woman became a mere Distillory for the production of the largest and most transparent tears I ever met with. Combined with these characteristics, was a peculiar tenacity of hold in those specimens, so that they didn't fall, but hung upon her face and nose. In this condition, and mildly and deplorably shaking her head, her silence would throw me more heavily than the Admirable Crichton could have done in a verbal disputation for a purse of money. Cook, likewise, always covered me with confusion as with a garment, by neatly winding up the session with the protest that the Ouse was wearing her out, and by meekly repeating her last wishes regarding her silver watch.

As to our nightly life, the contagion of suspicion and fear was among us, and there is no such contagion under the sky. Hooded woman? According to the accounts, we were in a perfect Convent of hooded women. Noises? With that contagion downstairs, I myself have sat in the dismal parlour, listening, until I have heard so many and such strange noises, that they would have chilled my blood if I had not warmed it by dashing out to make discoveries. Try this in bed, in the dead of the night; try this at your own comfortable fireside, in the life of the night. You can fill any house with noises, if you will, until you have a noise for every nerve in your nervous system.

I repeat; the contagion of suspicion and fear was among us, and there is no such contagion under the sky. The women (their noses in a chronic state of excoriation from smelling-salts) were always primed and loaded for a swoon, and ready to go off with hair-triggers. The two elder detached the Odd Girl on all expeditions that were considered doubly hazardous, and she always established the reputation of such adventures by coming back cateleptic. If Cook or Streaker went overhead after dark, we knew we should presently hear a bump on the ceiling; and this took place so constantly, that it was as if a fighting man were engaged to go about the house, adminstering a touch of his art which I believe is called The Auctioneer, to every domestic he met with.

It was in vain to do anything. It was in vain to be frightened, for the moment in one's own person, by a real owl, and then to show the owl. It was in vain to discover, by striking an accidental discord on the piano, that Turk always howled at particular notes and combinations. It was in vain to be a Rhadamanthus with the bells, and if an unfortunate bell rang without leave, to have it down inexorably and silence it. It was in vain to fire up chimneys, let torches down the well, charge furiously into suspected rooms and recesses. We changed servants, and it was no better. The new set ran away, and a third set came, and it was no better. At last, our comfortable housekeeping got to be so disorganised and wretched, that I one night dejectedly said to my sister: 'Patty, I begin to despair of our getting people to go on with us here, and I think we must give this up.'

My sister, who is a woman of immense spirit, replied, 'No, John, don't give it up. Don't be beaten, John. There is another way.'

'And what is that?' said I.

'John,' returned my sister, 'if we are not to be driven out of this house, and that for no reason whatever, that is apparent to you or me, we must help ourselves and take the house wholly and solely into our own hands.'

'But, the servants,' said I.

'Have no servants,' said my sister, boldly.

Like most people in my grade of life, I had never thought of the possibility of going on without those faithful obstructions. The notion was so new to me when suggested, that I looked very doubtful.

'We know they come here to be frightened and infect one another, and we know they are frightened and do infect one another,' said my sister.

'With the exception of Bottles,' I observed, in a meditative tone.

(The deaf stable-man. I kept him in my service, and still keep him, as a phenomenon of moroseness not to be matched in England.)

'To be sure, John,' assented by sister; 'except Bottles. And what does that go to prove? Bottles talks to nobody, and hears nobody unless he is absolutely roared at, and what alarm has Bottles ever given, or taken? None.'

This was perfectly true; the individual in question having retired, every night at ten o'clock, to his bed over the coach-house, with no other company than a pitchfork and a pail of water. That the pail of water would have been over me, and the pichfork through me, if I had put myself without announcement in Bottles's way after that minute, I had deposited in my own mind as a fact worth remembering. Neither had Bottles ever taken the least notice of any of our many uproars. An imperturbable and speechless man, he had sat at his supper, with Streaker present in a swoon, and the Odd Girl marble, and had only put another potato in his cheek, or profited by the general misery to help himself to beefsteak pie.

'And so,' continued my sister, 'I exempt Bottles. And considering, John, that the house is too large, and perhaps too lonely, to be kept well in hand by Bottles, you, and me, I propose that we cast about among our friends for a certain selected number of the most reliable and willing – form a Society here for three months – wait upon ourselves and one another – live cheerfully and socially – and see what happens.'

I was so charmed with my sister, that I embraced her on the spot, and went into her plan with the greatest ardour.

We were then in the third week of November; but, we took our measures so vigorously, and were so well seconded by the friends in whom we confided, that there was still a week of the month unexpired, when our party all came down together merrily, and mustered in the haunted house.

I will mention, in this place, two small changes that I made while my sister and I were yet alone. It occurring to me as not improbable that Turk howled in the house of night, partly because he wanted to get out of it, I stationed him in his kennel outside, but unchained; and I seriously warned the village that any man who came in his way must not expect to leave him without a rip in his own throat. I then casually asked Ikey if he were a judge of a gun? On his saying, 'Yes, Sir, I knows a good gun when I sees her.' I begged the favour of his stepping up to the house and looking at mine.

'*She's* a true one, Sir,' said Ikey, after inspecting a double-barrelled rifle that I bought in New York a few years ago. 'No mistake about *her*, Sir.'

'Ikey,' said I, 'don't mention it; I have seen something in this house.'

'No, Sir?' he whispered, greedily opening his eyes. ''Ooded lady, Sir?'

'Don't be frightened,' said I. 'It was a figure rather like you.'

'Lord, Sir?'

'Ikey!' said I, shaking hands with him warmly: I may say affectionately; 'if there is any truth in these ghost-stories, the greatest service I can do you, is, to fire at that figure. And I promise you, by Heaven and earth, I will do it with this gun if I see it again!'

The young man thanked me, and took his leave with some little precipitation, after declining a glass of liquor. I imparted my secret to him, because I had never quite forgotten his throwing his cap at the bell; because I had, on another occasion, noticed something very like a fur cap, lying not far from the bell, one night when it had burst out ringing; and because I had remarked that we were at our ghostliest whenever he came up in the evening to comfort the servants. Let me do Ikey no injustice. He was afraid of the house, and believed in its being haunted; and yet he would play false on the haunting side, so surely as he got an opportunity. The Odd Girl's case was exactly similar. She went about the house in a state of real terror, and yet lied monstrously and wilfully, and invented many of the alarms she spread, and made many of the sounds we heard. I had had my eye on the two, and I know it. It is not necessary for me, here to account for this preposterous state of mind; I content myself with remarking that it is familiarly known to every intelligent man who has had fair medical, legal, or other watchful experience; that it is as well established and as common a state of mind as any with which observers are acquainted; and that it is one of the first elements, above all others, rationally to be suspected in, and strictly looked for, and separated from, any question of this kind.

To return to our party. The first thing we did when we were all assembled, was, to draw lots for bedrooms. That done, and every bedroom, and indeed, the whole house, having been minutely examined by the whole body, we allotted the various household duties, as if we had been on a gipsy party, or a yachting party, or a hunting party, or were shipwrecked. I then recounted the floating rumours concerning the hooded lady, the owl, and Master B.: with others, still more filmy, which had floated about during our occupation, relative to some ridiculous old ghost of the female gender who went up and down, carrying the ghost of a round table; and also to an impalpable Jackass, whom nobody was ever able to catch. Some of these ideas I really believe our people below had communicated to one another in some diseased way, without conveying them in words. We then gravely called one another to witness, that we were not there to be deceived, or to deceive – which we considered pretty much the same thing – and that, with a serious sense of responsibility, we would be strictly true to one another, and would strictly follow out the truth. The understanding was established, that any one who heard unusual noises in the night, and who wished to trace them, should knock at my door; lastly, that on Twelfth Night, the last night of holy Christmas, all our individual experiences since that then present hour of our coming together in the haunted house, should be brought to light for the good of all; and that we would hold our peace on the subject till then, unless on some remarkable provocation to break silence.

We were, in number and in character, as follows:

First – to get my sister and myself out of the way – there were we two. In the drawing of lots, my sister drew her own room, and I drew Master B.'s. Next, there was our first cousin John Herschel, so called after the great astronomer: than whom I suppose a better man at a telescope does not breathe. With him, was his wife: a charming creature to whom he had been married in the previous spring. I thought him (under the circumstances) rather imprudent to bring her, because there is no knowing what even a false alarm may do at such a time; but I suppose he knew his own business best, and I must say that if she had been *my* wife, I never could have left her endearing and bright face behind. They drew the Clock Room. Alfred Starling, an uncommonly agreeable young fellow of eight-and-twenty for whom I have the greatest liking, was in the Double Room; mine, usually, and designated by that name from having a dressing-room within it, with two large and cumbersome windows, which no wedges I was ever able to make, would keep from shaking, in any weather, wind or no wind. Alfred is a young fellow who pretends to be 'fast' (another word for loose, as I understand the term), but who is much too good and sensible for that nonsense, and who would have distinguished himself before now, if his father had not unfortunately left him a small independence of two hundred a year, on the strength of which his only occupation in life has been to spend six. I am in hopes, however, that this Banker may break, or that he may enter into some speculation guaranteed to pay twenty per cent.; for, I am convinced that if he could only be ruined, his fortune is made. Belinda Bates, bosom friend of my sister, and a most intellectual, amiable, and delightful girl, got the Picture Room. She has a fine genius for poetry, combined with real business earnestness, and 'goes in' – to use an expression of Alfred's – for Woman's mission, Woman's rights, Woman's wrongs, and everything that is woman's with a capital W, or is not and ought to be, or is and ought not to be. 'Most praiseworthy, my dear, and Heaven prosper yet!' I whispered to her on the first night of my taking leave of her at the Picture-Room door, 'but don't overdo it. And in respect of the great necessity there is, my darling, for more employ-ments being within the reach of Woman than our civilisation has as yet assigned to her, don't fly at the unfortunate men, even those men who are at first sight in your way, as if they were the natural oppressors of your sex; for, trust me, Belinda, they do sometimes spend their wages amoung wives and daughters, sisters, mothers, aunts, and grandmothers; and the play is, really, not *all* Wolf and Red Riding-Hood, but has other parts in it.' However, I digress.

Belinda, as I have mentioned, occupied the Picture Room. We had but three chambers: the Corner Room, the Cupboad Room, and the Garden Room. My old friend, Jack Governor, 'slung his hammock,' as he called it, in the Corner Room. I have always regarded Jack as the finest-looking sailor that ever sailed. He is gray now, but as handsome as he was a quarter of a century ago – nay, handsomer. A portly, cheery, well-built figure of a broad-shouldered man, with a frank smile, as brilliant dark eye, and a rich dark eyebrow. I remember those under darker hair, and they look all the better for their silver setting. He has been wherever his Union namesake flies, has Jack, and I have met old shipmates of his, away in the Mediterranean and on the other side of the Atlantic, who have beamed and brightened at the casual mention of this name, and have cried, 'You know Jack Governor? Then you know a prince of men!' That he is! And so unmistakably a naval officer, that if you were to meet him coming out of an Esquimaux snow-hut in seal's skins, you would be vaguely persuaded he was in full naval uniform.

Jack once had that bright clear eye of his on my sister; but, it fell out that he married another lady and took her to South America, where she died. This was a dozen years ago or more. He brought down with him to our haunted house a little cask of salt beef; for, he is always convinced that all salt beef not of his own pickling, is mere carrion, and invariably, when he goes to London, packs a piece in his portmanteau. He had also volunteered to bring with him one 'Nat Beaver,' an old comrade of his, captain of a merchantman. Mr. Beaver, with a thick-set wooden face and figure, and apparently as hard as a block all over, proved to be an intelligent man, with a world of watery experiences in him, and great practical knowledge. At times, there was a curious nervousness about him, apparently the lingering result of some old illness; but, it seldom lasted many minutes. He got the Cupboard Room, and lay there next to Mr. Undery, my friend and solicitor: who came down, in an amateur capacity, 'to go through with it,' as he said, and who plays whist better than the whole Law List, from the red cover at the beginning to the red cover at the end.

I never was happier in my life, and I believe it was the universal feeling among us. Jack Governor, always a man of wonderful resources, was Chief Cook, and made some of the best dishes I ever ate, including unapproachable curries. My sister was pastrycook and confectioner. Starling and I were Cook's Mate, turn and turn about, and on special occasions the chief cook 'pressed' Mr. Beaver. We had a great deal of out-door sport and exercise, but nothing was neglected within, and there was no ill-humour or misunderstanding among us, and our evenings were so delightful that we had at least one good reason for being reluctant to go to bed.

We had a few night alarms in the beginning. On the first night, I was knocked up by Jack with a most wonderful ship's lantern in his hand, like the gills of some monster of the deep, who informed me that he 'was going aloft to the main truck,' to have the weathercock down. It was a stormy night, and I remonstrated; but Jack called my attention to its making a sound like a cry of despair, and said somebody would be 'hailing a ghost' presently, if it wasn't done. So, up to the top of the house, where I could hardly stand for the wind, we went, accompanied by Mr. Beaver; and there Jack, lantern and all, with Mr. Beaver after him, swarmed up to the top of a cupola, some two dozen feet above the chimneys, and stood upon nothing particular, coolly knocking the weathercock off, until they both got into such good spirits with the wind and the height, that I thought they would never come down. Another night, they turned out again, and had a chimney-cowl off. Another night, they cut a sobbing and gulping water-pipe away. Another night, they found out something else. On several occasions, they both, in the coolest manner, simultaneously dropped out of their respective bedroom windows, hand over hand by their counterpanes, to 'overhaul' something mysterious in the garden.

The engagement among us was faithfully kept, and nobody revealed anything. All we knew was, if any one's room were haunted, no one looked the worse for it.

THE GHOST IN MASTER B.'S ROOM

When I established myself in the triangular garret which had gained so distinguished a reputation, my thoughts naturally turned to Master B. My speculations about him were uneasy and manifold. Whether his Christian name was Benjamin, Bissextile (from his having been born in Leap Year), Bartholomew, or Bill. Whether the initial letter belonged to his family name, and that was Baxter, Black, Brown, Barker, Buggins, Baker, or Bird. Whether he was a foundling, and had been baptized B. Whether he was a lion-hearted boy, and B. was short for Briton, or for Bull. Whether he could possibly have been kith and kin to an illustrious lady who brightened my own childhood, and had come of the blood of the brilliant Mother Bunch?

With these profitless meditations I tormented myself much. I also carried the mysterious letter into the appearance and pursuits of the deceased; wondering whether he dressed in Blue, wore Boots (he couldn't have been Bald), was a boy of Brains, liked Books, was good at Bowling, had any skill as a Boxer, even in his Buoyant Boyhood Bathed from a Bathing-machine at Bognor, Bangor, Bournemouth, Brighton, or Broadstairs, like a Bounding Billiard Ball?

So, from the first, I was haunted by the letter B.

It was not long before I remarked that I never by any hazard had a dream of Master B., or of anything belonging to him. But, the instant I awoke from sleep, at whatever hour of the night, my thoughts took him up, and roamed away, trying to attach his initial letter to something that would fit it and keep it quiet.

For six nights, I had been worried thus in Master B.'s room, when I began to perceive that things were going wrong.

The first appearance that presented itself was early in the morning when it was but just daylight and no more. It was standing shaving at my glass, when I suddenly discovered, to

my consternation and amazement, that I was shaving – not
myself – I am fifty – but a boy. Apparently Master B.!

I trembled and looked over my shoulder; nothing there. I
looked again in the glass, and distinctly saw the features and
expression of a boy, who was shaving, not to get rid of a
beard, but to get one. Extremely troubled in my mind, I took
a few turns in the room, and went back to the looking-glass,
resolved to steady my hand and complete the operation in
which I had been disturbed. Opening my eyes, which I had
shut while recovering my firmness, I now met in the glass,
looking straight at me, the eyes of a young man of four or five
and twenty. Terrified by this new ghost, I closed my eyes, and
made a strong effort to recover myself. Opening them again, I
saw, shaving his cheek in the glass, my father, who has long
been dead. Nay, I even saw my grandfather too, whom I
never did see in my life.

Although naturally much affected by these remarkable
visitations, I determined to keep my secret, until the time
agreed upon for the present general disclosure. Agitated by a
multitude of curious thoughts, I retired to my room, that
night, prepared to encounter some new experience of a
spectral character. Nor was my preparation needless, for,
waking from an uneasy sleep at exactly two o'clock in the
morning, what were my feelings to find that I was sharing my
bed with the skeleton of Master B.!

I sprang up, and the skeleton sprang up also. I then heard a
plaintive voice saying, 'Where am I! What is become of me?'
and, looking hard in that direction, perceived the ghost of
Master B.

The young spectre was dressed in an obsolete fashion: or
rather, was not so much dressed as put into a case of inferior
pepper-and-salt cloth, made horrible by means of shining
buttons. I observed that these buttons went, in a double row,
over each shoulder of the young ghost, and appeared to
descend his back. He wore a frill round his neck. His right
hand (which I distinctly noticed to be inky) was laid upon his
stomach; connecting this action with some feeble pimples on
his countenance, and his general air of nausea, I concluded this
ghost to be the ghost of a boy who had habitually taken a great
deal too much medicine.

'Where am I?' said the little spectre, in a pathetic voice. 'And why was I born in the Calomel days, and why did I have all that Calomel given me?'

I replied, with sincere earnestness, that upon my soul I couldn't tell him.

'Where is my little sister,' said the ghost, 'and where my angelic little wife, and where is the boy I went to school with?'

I entreated the phantom to be comforted, and above all things to take heart respecting the loss of the boy he went to school with. I represented to him that probably that boy never did, within human experience, come out well, when discovered. I urged that I myself had, in later life, turned up several boys whom I went to school with, and none of them had at all answered. I expressed my humble belief that the boy never did answer. I represented that he was a mythic character, a delusion, and a snare. I recounted how, the last time I found him, I found him at a dinner party behind a wall of white cravat, with an inconclusive opinion on every possible subject, and a power of silent boredom absolutely Titanic. I related how, on the strength of our having been together at 'Old Doylance's,' he had asked himself to breakfast with me (a social offence of the largest magnitude); how, fanning my weak embers of belief in Doylance's boys, I had let him in; and how, he had proved to be a fearful wanderer about the earth, pursuing the race of Adam with inexplicable notions concerning the currency, and with a proposition that the Bank of England should, on pain of being abolished, instantly strike off and circulate, God knows how many thousand millions of ten-and-sixpenny notes.

The ghost heard me in silence, and with a fixed stare. 'Barber!' it apostrophised me when I had finished.

'Barber?' I repeated – for I am not of that profession.

'Condemned,' said the ghost, 'to shave a constant change of customers – now, me – now, a young man – now, thyself as thou art – now, thy father – now, thy grandfather; condemned, too, to lie down with a skeleton every night, and to rise with it every morning –'

(I shuddered on hearing this dismal announcement).

'Barber! Pursue me!'

I had felt, even before the words were uttered, that I was

under a spell to pursue the phantom. I immediately did so, and was in Master B.'s room no longer.

Most people knew what long and fatiguing night journeys had been forced upon the witches who used to confess, and who, no doubt, told the exact truth – particularly as they were always assisted with leading questions, and the Torture was always ready. I asseverate that, during my occupation of Master B.'s room, I was taken by the ghost that haunted it, on expeditions fully as long and wild as any of those. Assuredly, I was presented to no shabby old man with a goat's horns and tail (something between Pan and an old clothesman), holding conventional receptions, as stupid as those of real life and less decent; but, I came upon other things which appeared to me to have more meaning.

Confident that I speak the truth and shall be believed, I declare without hesitation that I followed the ghost, in the first instance on a broom-stick, and afterwards on a rocking-horse. The very smell of the animal's paint – especially when I brought it out, by making him warm – I am ready to swear to. I followed the ghost, afterwards, in a hackney coach; an institution with the peculiar smell of which, the present generation is unacquainted, but to which I am again ready to swear as a combination of stable, dog with the mange, and very old bellows. (In this, I appeal to previous generations to confirm or refute me.) I pursued the phantom, on a headless donkey: at least, upon a donkey who was so interested in the state of his stomach that his head was always down there, investigating it; on ponies, expressly born to kick up behind; on roundabouts and swings, from fairs; in the first cab – another forgotten institution where the fare regularly got into bed, and was tucked up with the driver.

Not to trouble you with a detailed account of all my travels in pursuit of the ghost of Master B., which were longer and more wonderful than those of Sinbad the Sailor, I will confine myself to one experience from which you may judge of many.

I was marvellously changed. I was myself, yet not myself. I was conscious of something within me, which has been the same all through my life, and which I have always recognised under all its phases and varieties as never altering, and yet I was not the I who had gone to bed in Master B.'s room. I had the smoothest of faces and the shortest of legs, and I had taken another creature like myself, also with the smoothest of faces and the shortest of legs, behind a door, and was confiding to him a proposition of the most astounding nature.

This proposition was, that we should have a Seraglio.

The other creature assented warmly. He had no notion of respectability, neither had I. It was the custom of the East, it was the way of the good Caliph Haroun Alraschid (let me have the corrupted name again for once, it is so scented with sweet memories!), the usage was highly laudable, and most worthy of imitation. 'O, yes! Let us,' said the other creature with a jump, 'have a Seraglio.'

It was not because we entertained the faintest doubts of the meritorious character of the Oriental establishment we proposed to import, that we perceived it must be kept a secret from Miss Griffin. It was because we knew Miss Griffin to be bereft of human sympathies, and incapable of appreciating the greatness of the great Haroun. Mystery impenetrably shrouded from Miss Griffin then, let us entrust it to Miss Bule.

We were ten in Miss Griffin's establishment by Hampstead Ponds; eight ladies and two gentlemen. Miss Bule, whom I judged to have attained the ripe age of eight or nine, took the lead in society. I opened the subject to her in the course of the day, and proposed that she should become the Favourite.

Miss Bule, after struggling with the diffidence so natural to, and charming in, her adorable sex, expressed herself as flattered by the idea, but wished to know how it was proposed to provide for Miss Pipson? Miss Bule – who was understood to have vowed towards that young lady, a friendship, halves, and no secrets, until death, on the Church Service and Lessons complete in two volumes with case and lock – Miss Bule said she could not, as the friend of Pipson, disguise from herself, or me, that Pipson was not one of the common.

Now, Miss Pipson, having curly light hair and blue eyes (which was my idea of anything mortal and feminine that was called Fair), I promptly replied that I regarded Miss Pipson in the light of a Fair Circassian.

'And what then?' Miss Bule pensively asked.

I replied that she must be inveigled by a Merchant, brought to me veiled, and purchased as a slave.

[The other creature had already fallen into the second male place in the State, and was set apart for Grand Vizier. He afterwards resisted this disposal of events, but had his hair pulled until he yielded.]

'Shall I not be jealous?' Miss Bule inquired, casting down her eyes.

'Zobeide, no,' I replied; 'you will ever be the favourite Sultana; the first place in my heart, and on my throne, will be ever yours.'

Miss Bule, upon that assurance, consented to propound the idea to her seven beautiful companions. It occurring to me, in the course of the same day, that we knew we could trust a grinning and good-natured soul called Tabby, who was the serving drudge of the house, and had no more figure than one of the beds, and upon whose face there was always more or less black-lead, I slipped into Miss Bule's hand after supper, a little note to that effect: dwelling on the black-lead as being in a manner deposited by the finger of Providence, pointing Tabby out for Mesrour, the celebrated chief of the Blacks of the Hareem.

There were difficulties in the formation of the desired institution, as there are in all combinations. The other creature showed himself of a low character, and, when defeated in aspiring to the throne, pretended to have conscientious scruples about prostrating himself before the Caliph; wouldn't call him Commander of the Faithful; spoke of him slightingly and inconsistently as a mere 'chap;' said he, the other creature, 'wouldn't play' – Play! and was otherwise coarse and offensive. This meanness of disposition was, however, put down by the general indignation of an united Seraglio, and I became blessed in the smiles of eight of the fairest of the daughters of men.

The smiles could only be bestowed when Miss Griffin was looking another way, and only then in very wary manner, for there was a legend among the followers of the Prophet that she saw with a little round ornament in the middle of the pattern on the back of her shawl. But every day after dinner, for an hour, we were all together, and then the Favourite and the rest of the Royal Hareem competed who should most beguile the leisure of the Serene Haroun reposing from the cares of State –

which were generally, as in most affairs of State, of an arithmetical character, the Commander of the Faithful being a fearful boggler at a sum.

On these occasions, the devoted Mesrour, chief of the Blacks of the Hareem, was always in attendance (Miss Griffin usually ringing for that officer, at the same time, with great vehemence), but never acquitted himself in a manner worthy of his historical reputation. In the first place, his bringing a broom into the Divan of the Caliph, even when Haroun wore on his shoulders the red robe of anger (Miss Pipson's pelisse), though it might be got over for the moment, was never to be quite satisfactorily accounted for. In the second place, his breaking out into grinning exclamations of 'Lork you pretties!' was neither Eastern nor respectful. In the third place, when specially instructed to say 'Bismillah!' he always said 'Hallelujah!' This officer, unlike his class, was too good-humoured altogether, kept his mouth open far too wide, expressed approbation to an incongruous extent, and even once – it was on the occasion of the purchase of the Fair Circassian for five hundred thousand purses of gold, and cheap, too – embraced the Slave, the Favourite, and the Caliph, all round. (Parenthetically let me say God bless Mesrour, and may there have been sons and daughters on that tender bosom, softening many a hard day since!)

Miss Griffin was a model of propriety, and I am at a loss to imagine what the feelings of the virtuous woman would have been, if she had known, when she paraded us down the Hampstead-road two and two, that she was walking with a stately step at the head of Polygamy and Mahomedanism. I believe that a mysterious and terrible joy with which the contemplation of Miss Griffin, in this unconscious state, inspired us, and a grim sense prevalent among us that there was a dreadful power in our knowledge of what Miss Griffin (who knew all things that could be learnt out of book) didn't know, were the mainspring of the preservation of our secret. It was wonderfully kept, but was once upon the verge of self-betrayal. The danger and escape occurred upon a Sunday. We were all ten ranged in a conspicuous part of the gallery at church, with Miss Griffin at our head – as we were every Sunday – advertising the establishment in an unsecular sort of way – when the description of Solomon in his domestic glory happened to be read. The moment that monarch was thus referred to, conscience whispered me, 'Thou, too, Haroun!' The officiating minister had a cast in his eye, and it assisted conscience by giving him the appearance of reading personally at me. A crimson blush, attended by a fearful perspiration, suffused my features. The Grand Vizier become more dead than alive, and the whole Seraglio reddened as if the sunset of Bagdad shone direct upon their lovely faces. At this portentous time the awful Griffin rose, and balefully surveyed the children of Islam. My own impression was, that Church and State had entered into a conspiracy with Miss Griffin to expose us, and that we should all be put into white sheets, and exhibited in the centre aisle. But, so Westerly – if I may be allowed the expression as opposite to Eastern associations – was Miss Griffin's sense of rectitude, that she merely suspected Apples, and we were saved.

I have called the Seraglio, united. Upon the question, solely, whether the Commander of the Faithful durst exercise a right of kissing in that sanctuary of the palace, were its peerless inmates divided. Zobeide asserted a counter-right in the Favourite to scratch, the fair Circassian put her face, for refuge, into a green baize bag, originally designed for books. On the other hand, a young antelope of transcendent beauty from the fruitful plains of Camdentown (whence she had been brought, by traders, in the half-yearly caravan that crossed the intermediate desert after the holidays), held more liberal opinions, but stipulated for limiting the benefit of them to that dog, and son of a dog, the Grand Vizier – who had no rights, and was not in question. At length, the difficulty was compromised by the installation of a very youthful slave as Deputy. She, raised upon a stool, officially received upon her cheeks the salutes intended by the gracious Haroun for other Sultanas, and was privately rewarded from the coffers of the Ladies of the Hareem.

And now it was, at the full height of enjoyment of my bliss, that I became heavily troubled. I began to think of my mother, and what she would say to my taking home at Midsummer eight of the most beautiful of the daughers of men, but all unexpected. I though of the number of beds we made up at our house, of my father's income, and of the baker, and my despondency redoubled. The Seraglio and malicious Vizier, divining the cause of their Lord's unhappiness, did their utmost to augment it. They professed unbounded fidelity, and declared that they would live and die with him. Reduced to the utmost wretchedness by these protestations of attachment, I lay awake, for hours at a time, ruminating on my frightful lot. In my despair, I think I might have taken an early opportunity of falling on my knees before Miss Griffin, avowing my resemblance to Solomon, and praying to be dealt with according to the outraged laws of my country, if an unthought-of means of escape had not opened before me.

One day, we were out walking, two and two – on which occasion the Vizier had his usual instructions to take note of the boy at the turnpike, and if he profanely gazed (which he always did) at the beauties of the Hareem, to have him bow-strung in the course of the night – and it happened that our hearts were veiled in gloom. An unaccountable action on the part of the antelope had plunged the State into disgrace. That charmer, on the representation that the previous day was her birthday, and that vast treasures had been sent in a hamper for its celebration (both baseless assertions), had secretly but most pressingly invited thirty-five neighbouring princes and princesses to a ball and supper: with a special stipulation that they were 'not to be fetched till twelve.' This wandering of the antelope's fancy, led to the surprising arrival at Miss Griffin's door, in divers equipages and under various escorts, of a great company in full dress, who were deposited on the top step in a flush of high expectancy, and who were dismissed in tears. At the beginning of the double knocks attendant on these ceremonies, the antelope had retired to a back attic, and bolted herself in; and at every new arrival Miss Griffin had gone so much more and more distracted, that at last she had been seeen to tear her front. Ultimate capitulation on the part of the offender, had been followed by solitude in the linen-closet, bread and water and a lecture to all, of vindictive length, in which Miss Griffin had used expressions: Firstly, 'I believe you all of you knew of it;' Secondly, 'Every one of you is as wicked as another;' Thirdly, 'A pack of little wretches.'

Under these circumstances, we were walking drearily

along; and I especially, with my Moosulmaun responsibilities
heavy on me, was in a very low state of mind; when a strange
man accosted Miss Griffin, and, after walking on at her side
for a little while and talking with her, looked at me. Suppos-
ing him to be a minion of the law, and that my hour was
come, I instantly ran away, with the general purpose of
making for Egypt.

The whole Seraglio cried out, when they saw me making
off as fast as my legs would carry me (I had an impression that
the first turning on the left, and round by the public-house,
would be the shortest way to the Pyramids), Miss Griffin
screamed after me, the faithless Vizier ran after me, and the
boy at the turnpike dodged me into a corner, like a sheep, and
cut me off. Nobody scolded me when I was taken and brought
back; Miss Griffin only said, with a stunning gentleness, This
was very curious! Why had I run away when the gentleman
looked at me?

If I had had any breath to answer with, I dare say I should
have made no to answer; having no breath, I certainly made
none. Miss Griffin and the strange man took me between
them, and walked me back to the palace in a sort of state; but
not at all (as I couldn't help feeling, with astonishment), in
culprit state.

When we got there, we went into a room by ourselves, and
Miss Griffin called in to her assistance, Mesrour, chief of the
dusky guards of the Hareem. Mesrour, on being whispered
to, began to shed tears.

'Bless you, my precious!' said that officer, turning to me;
'your pa's took bitter bad!'   \

I asked, with a fluttered heart, 'Is he very ill?'

'Lord temper the wind to you, my lamb!' said the good
Mesrour, kneeling down, that I might have a comforting
shoulder for my head to rest on, 'your pa's dead!'

Haroun Alraschid took to flight at the words; the Seraglio
vanished; from that moment, I never again saw one of the
eight of the fairest of the daughters of men.

I was taken home, and there was Debt at home as well as
Death, and we had a sale there. My own little bed was so
superciliously looked upon by a Power unknown to me,
hazily called 'The Trade,' that a brass coal-scuttle, a roasting-

jack, and a birdcage, were obliged to be put into it to make a
Lot of it, and then it went for a song. So I heard mentioned
and I wondered what song, and thought what a dismal song
it must have been to sing!

Then, I was sent to a great, cold, bare, school of big boys;
where everything to eat and wear was thick and clumpy,
without being enough; where everybody, large and small, was
cruel; where the boys knew all about the sale, before I got
there, and asked me what I had fetched, and who had bought
me, and hooted at me. 'Going, going, gone!' I never whispered in that wretched place that I had been Haroun or had had
a Seraglio: for, I knew that if I mentioned my reverses, I
should be so worried, that I should have to drown myself in
the muddy pond near the playground, which looked like the
beer.

Ah me, ah me! no other ghost has haunted the boy's room,
my friends, since I have occupied it, than the ghost of my own
childhood, the ghost of my own innocence, the ghost of my
own airy belief. Many a time have I pursued the phantom:
never with this man's stride of mine to come up with it, never
with these man's hands of mine to touch it, never more to this
man's heart of mine to hold it in its purity. And here you see
me working out, as cheerfully and thankfully as I may, my
doom of shaking in the glass a constant change of customers,
and of lying down and rising up with the skeleton allotted to
me for my mortal companion.